BUBBLES IN SPACE
TROPICAL PUNCH

First e-book edition: March 2021
Northern Edge Publishing
Hague, Saskatchewan, Canada

Cover design by Martin ® Cover Art Studio
www.coverartstudio.com

Formatted by Crafted by AF (IG/FB: @craftedbyaf)

www.scjensen.com

S.C. JENSEN

BUBBLES IN SPACE

TROPICAL PUNCH 1

This book is dedicated to Raymond Chandler and Dashiell Hammett.

Sorry guys, but it really is all your fault.

A NOTE ON LANGUAGE

Thank you for picking up a copy of **Bubbles in Space #1**: *Tropical Punch*!

This series is my personal homage to the American pulp noir writers of the early 20th century, with a neo-cyberpunk twist.

In this story, I've repurposed some of the slang popular in American pulp novels from the 1920s – 1940s. I have tried to make meanings clear with context, however, if you need clarification on any unfamiliar words, I have provided a glossary in the back with the original meanings and how they are used in HoloCity.

If you'd like to read more about Bubbles' adventures, join my VIP Readers Group to get a free copy of my novella *Dames for Hire*, which tells the story of her very first case as a HoloCity P.I.

Enjoy!

P.S. This novel has been written in Canadian English. This means it includes an infuriating blend of American vocabulary with British grammar and spellings.

So, sorry about that, eh? We're a little weird up here.

CHAPTER 1

I wove my way through the writhing dancers on the floor of techRose with my eyes on the girl. My skin pinched beneath the cybernetic prosthetic on my left shoulder. It was time for a refit. Should have thought of that before heading out on the job, but I didn't expect it to be a problem.

Find the girl, deliver the message. Easy enough.

The girl's hair didn't match, not black enough, but hair didn't cost much to change. She was about the right shape and size to be the one my client was looking for. Petite and dark-skinned, with a silver dress that left only modesty to the imagination. The hair—purple now, not black at all—bounced hypnotically with her hips and faded to pink.

A wig.

I reached out to touch her shoulder with my real arm, and she spun slowly like a display mannequin in an all-night sex shop. A skim of sweat shimmered on her forehead and the wig pulsed yellow and green with the bass rumbling through the floor. Swollen black pupils stared out from beneath metallic-white paint, the frosted lashes so thick she could hardly keep her eyes open.

No necklace.

The air, greasy with sweat and glitter, stuck to my throat. She wasn't my girl, but I might still get some answers out of her. "You look like you could use a drink."

Closer to the stage, music ground my eardrums with more passion than the boys up in the go-go boxes. The girls on stage gave their poles the juice, though, and HoloCity credit chips flew through the air like confetti.

She blinked up at me and licked her black painted lips. "You buying?"

She didn't mean drinks, but I led her out of the crowd toward the bar anyway. This time I used my other arm, the metal one, to part the swath of writhing bodies. It earned me some dirty looks, but no one wanted to pick a fight with a chick with a robotic fist.

Sheets of corrugated metal had been welded together and painted with cheap pink holographic paint to make up the bar. The paint had chipped off in rusty scabs and it crumpled in on the side nearest the entrance, probably where the bouncers had gotten a little too excited about their jobs. Class joint, techRose.

I hailed the barkeep with my cybernetic arm just to show him I had money. I didn't, not much, but tech prosthetics don't come cheap—even ugly ones like mine, with all the metal bones and tendons exposed like a silver skeleton, that pinch when you move. Anyway, it wouldn't hurt him to make some assumptions. I said, "Get her something to sober her up."

"You're not buying," she said. Disappointment tugged her lips into a pout, pretty if you like them slack-jawed and bleary-eyed.

"Just drinks."

The bartender, a skinny faced weasel with the sallow complexion of a man who sampled too much of his own wares after hours, swung a glass of noxious green liquid toward the girl. He turned his carefully bored expression on me. "And you?"

"Give me a shot of the pure stuff." I held out my chipped hand to pay for the transaction. "Tall glass."

His eyes had all the colour and life of a wrung-out dishrag, but this got his attention. "How pure?"

"The purest." I snapped my fingers. "I have the credits."

He narrowed his eyes and scanned my wrist. The till screen lit up green and he slunk off to the back room where they hid all the stuff that doesn't kill you. At the sunken end of the bar, he tipped his nose at someone and jerked his head a bit, just before he swung open the tetanus-riddled door to the back room.

"You're Bubbles Marlowe." The girl's eyes were a little less dead now that the drink had hit her, but as the glow-up left her cheeks a hollow, soulless look replaced it. "I'm not supposed to talk to you."

"You don't have to talk." I flashed her a 'gram from the tattler embedded in my metal arm. "Just nod your head. You know this girl?"

"You're not supposed to be here," she said, just loudly enough for anyone else who might be listening. She ducked her chin faintly and finished her drink.

The barkeep sidled back up to us and dropped a dirty glass filled with scuzzy-looking tap water in front of me. Best of the best. It probably cost me a week's wages.

He looked from the girl to the glass and to me again and grinned with pink gums and long teeth. "Expensive taste."

"She's not buying, Sy." The girl slid off her stool and almost crumpled. I caught her arm. Nothing like sobering up to realize how pinched you are. She steadied herself and pulled away from me. "I'm going up for a bit. Gotta fix my head."

Sy leered at her as she swayed toward the stairs to the dressing rooms. Then he turned to serve a big guy grunting into the seat next to me. The girl looked over her shoulder once and twitched her eyes toward the stairs before slipping back into the writhing crowd. Sober or not, she had a job to do. I tossed back the last of my water and started to slide off my stool to hit the stairs.

"What's the smoke, Bubbles?" a well-gravelled voice rumbled beside me.

I winced and turned to face the lump of flesh beside me. Grey eyes—eyes I once found irresistible—appraised me. He smirked. I resisted the urge to poke him with my metal fingers. I said, "Detective Weiland. You slumming it with the pinches tonight?"

"You used to call me Tom." He had the wide, easy mouth of an orator. A politician's smile. He wouldn't be a detective for long with a face like that. "When we were partners."

Weiland's rounded shoulders and barrel chest stretched out the shiny black button-down shirt he always wore undercover. His imitation-denim pants looked like he'd just paid a mint for them and forgotten to take off the tags. Probably it was the only outfit in his closet that wasn't the stark-grey HoloCity PD uniform.

"Things change." I spun towards him and rested my flesh-and-blood elbow on the bar. "Plasma rifles explode, arms burn off, partners get canned."

Weiland took a punch of his drink and bunched up the skin around his grey eyes like he was smiling. He spoke through his glass. "Ex-cops on disability buy cybernetic prostheses and forget to file their licence with government services."

"That why you're on me?" I hit the tattler again and flashed him my numbers. "I've got a ticket."

"You've probably got more tickets than you need." He set his glass on the bar between us and leaned back on his stool until the metal screamed its protest. "That's not why I'm here."

"If you're going to throw me a retirement party, you're about a year too late."

Weiland waved the bartender over and pushed his glass over the counter's chipped paint. The pink holographic surface looked sludgy in his shadow. The bartender flashed his weasel teeth and topped up Weiland's glass.

Weiland tipped his glass towards mine and clinked the rims. "You still hitting the hard stuff?"

The bartender sneered, and I covered my glass with my hand. "H_2O."

Weiland whistled. "Too rich for my blood."

"C_2H_6O doesn't roll off the tongue like it used to." I slid a hand into the breast pocket of my white, synth-leather vest and took out a piece of bright-pink chewing gum.

"Where'd you get the cush, Bubbles?" Weiland's eyes hardened. "I hope you're not overstepping your line."

I raised my eyebrows. "Gum's not that expensive, Detective. Even for us skids."

"The arm, Bubbles. An enhancement like that is worth a lot of dough. If you're taking dirty money from the wrong kind of people, Chief Swain's not going to be happy. I hope your business license is legit at least."

"Sure. Swain only likes dirty money when it's in his own pockets." I folded the gum against my tongue and pulled it into my mouth, biting hard. I chewed for a few seconds and then let him scan my P.I. ticket. "It's sweet that you're concerned. But I keep my nose clean."

The music thumped hard enough to ripple the amber surface of Weiland's drink. He spun the glass on the surface of the bar and gave me his cop stare. "By whose standards?"

I slid off my stool and stepped back out of the reach of his meat hooks. "It's not a drug case."

"Who's the pro skirt?" Weiland tipped his head toward the stairs.

I gnawed on the gum and shrugged. "Not who I hoped she was."

"You're pretty clammed up for someone with a clean nose." Weiland dropped to his feet and stepped a little closer. His pores oozed sweat and he reeked of cologne. Designer stuff applied with the delicate touch of a sledgehammer. "You sure there's nothing you want to tell me?"

"My clients have a right to their privacy."

Weiland held out his chip, but the bartender waved him away. His dishrag gaze had a practiced, saggy look, but his big ears twitched. "On the house, Detective."

Weiland dropped his arm without acknowledging the weasel-faced man beside him. He stared into my eyes and bent his bull-thick neck toward me and grinned. I didn't flinch.

"I'd like to believe you, Bubbles." He reached for my shoulder with a hand that could swallow my face and picked a piece of glitter off my vest. My hands balled into fists, and a nerve twinged in my left shoulder, but I stood still. He wiped the glitter on the end of my nose and tugged a strand of my chin-length, pink hair. "You look good. I don't want to have to mess you up."

"I made a promise, and I've kept it."

"Let's hope your word is as good as your dye job." Weiland stepped out of my airspace, and I breathed in a refreshing lungful of sweaty pheromones. "We're watching you."

He made his way for the exit like a shiny black iceberg, slow and insistent. The drunks and pinches stumbled and fell out of his way in a wave of technicoloured confusion. When I was sure he had left the building, I went for the stairs.

The bartender's nasal voice cut through the throbbing bassline. "What about my tip?"

I flipped him a metallic finger and pushed my way into the crush of bodies. The back stairs were a narrow tunnel of dirty black paint and suggestive graffiti that glowed under the club lights like holographic PornoPop ads. I had no burning desire to see what kind of sleazy digs the techRose pros were working, but if my girl was up there, I'd plug my nose and like it just fine.

A couple of glam boys were sucking on each other's faces on the staircase. I grabbed the top one and hauled them out of my way with my upgrade. They stuck together like mollusks and didn't miss a beat when I shoved them back into the crowd. An androgynous person with a shaved head and a long pink robe peered at me from the shadows of the tunnel. A puddle of questionable liquid pooled at the base of the stairs. I wrapped my metal fingers around the rail and hoisted myself over it and onto the third step.

Something caught my vest and yanked me backwards. I twisted just far enough to land on both feet in the ooze. Perfectly good pair of treads, ruined. A mug that was all jaw glowered down at me with piggy little eyes squinting out of folds of pasty pink flesh. The bouncer let go of my vest and grabbed the front of my shirt.

"That's her, Bug." A greasy little man peeked out from behind the thug's elbow. "Show her the street."

The bouncer blinked his eyes at me and seemed like he was thinking about it. I put my hands up. "C'mon, LeRoy. Call off your goon. I've got a job to do."

"You've got a hell of a lot of nerve, Marlowe." LeRoy Lemieux was five feet of fury wrapped up in an orange suit that screamed louder than techRose's sound system. He bounced on his toes like Terra Firma's tiniest prizefighter and bulged his pumped-up amphetamine eyes at me. "I seen you chatting up that slick dick detective. I seen it with my own eyes."

The thug twisted his fingers into my shirt, making it hard to breathe.

"I'm not working with the PD, LeRoy." I tugged at the bouncer's hand with my soft fingers and let the prosthesis hang limply at my side. No need to flash my goods if I didn't have to. LeRoy couldn't afford security goons with all their neural pistons firing, let alone with cybernetic upgrades. I didn't want to hurt the idiot. "Even if I wanted to, they wouldn't have me."

"I don't need your kinda trouble in my club, sister." An oily black curl broke free of LeRoy's coif and dangled between his jumpy black eyes. "I seen you, and I don't like what I seen. Show the lady the pavement, Bug. Let her feel it."

The bouncer blinked again and grunted. The command finally hit the lump of flesh inside his cranium, and he heaved me off the ground. My boots dangled above the puddle, dripping electric green bile. The goon turned slowly, like he wasn't quite sure where he was supposed to be going with his load. LeRoy spun on his heels and twitched his way toward the exit, his suit glowing like a pylon.

A shriek like tearing metal ricocheted down the stairwell toward us, and the bouncer paused. LeRoy whipped his greasy head around and hit me with a beady-eyed glare. His eyes twitched to the top of the stairs and then back to me. LeRoy vibrated on the spot, torn between competing urges. The lunk couldn't be trusted to find the door on his own, but that scream had come from his merchandise.

I swung my prosthesis into the bouncer's kidney and gave him a little extra hydraulic kick for fun. His maw opened like the gates of hell, and a burst of air like the off-gas from an outhouse hit me in the face. The piggy eyes disappeared into slimy pink folds of flesh, and the bouncer dropped like a lump of putty onto the grimy floor. I hit the ground running. LeRoy reacted fast, but when he tried to cut past me, I let him kiss the wall. The phantom arm beneath the cybernetic one screamed in protest. I ignored it, dodging glow-ups and dazed dancers like a pinball pro.

Another shriek tore through the techno pounding from the dance floor. Clubbers near the stairwell glanced vaguely at the corridor and shuffled their way into the crowd and away from the action. An orange blur slipped by on my left, and I reached for him with metal fingers. Missed. But LeRoy's heels slid in the puddle at the bottom of the stairwell, and I hit him hard from behind. I launched myself over his prone body with a boot on his narrow shoulder, plastering him into the steps.

A pale-skinned girl with white hair and barely enough clothes to dress a doll scrambled down the stairs toward us. Mascara-black tears streaked down her face like claw marks, and she grabbed onto my vest with long, silver fingernails, screaming.

"She's dead!" The girl dropped onto the stairs, dragging at my collar with her painted talons. "Somebody killed her. She's dead."

I picked the girl up and pushed her into LeRoy where he was peeling himself off the stairs. He went down in the slime again, shouting, "Stop her. Bug, you idiot, what am I paying you for? Stop her!"

But I was way ahead of them. I flew through the glowing, black tunnel toward the dressing rooms with a sick feeling in my chest.

It was my girl, I knew it.

It was my girl and I was too late.

CHAPTER 2

The second floor of techRose had as much charm as the first, minus the light show. Black lights on the peeling holographic paint left dull smears of reality poking through to remind customers that they could buy a pretty piece for a few hours, but underneath it all, they were just fleshy smudges in the technoglitter. It gave me the creeps, and I hadn't even dished out holocred for the privilege of this visit. A lingering haze of smoke blurred my vision and made the place look like a bad simulation.

The hallway at the top of the stairs had the smell of a locker room that hadn't seen the wet end of a mop in decades. Despite the ruckus the white-haired girl had kicked up, some punters still grunted away behind closed doors. At the end of the hallway, a thin triangle of red light broke through the gloom. A shadow flickered across it. I pressed myself against the wall and made a mental note to book myself a spa date in the decontamination unit. The floor thumped with the music downstairs, but the sound was thick and dirty. I sidled toward the opening, scanning the hallway for other cracked doors.

LeRoy, minus his lump of muscle, stood at the top of the stairs. He bounced on his toes and watched me with his twitchy, amped up gaze. Suddenly it didn't seem to be such a bad idea to let me make the first move. I let him stay there, blocking the only easy exit like a tube of nervous orange energy. If I scared up the perp, maybe knocking over the glow stick would slow him down long enough for me to catch him.

A rustling noise inside the room snapped my attention back to the door. I pressed myself against the jamb and held up my mech arm as if I had a gun in it. Old habits died hard. I hadn't touched a firearm since the accident. Until that moment, I hadn't had the sense to miss the old boom stick. I cursed myself silently and then peered around the corner.

A long-legged body lay sprawled on the floor in a pool of red light that turned her silver dress pink and the pool of blood black. A mirrored ball spun on the ceiling, sending motes of pale-rose light spinning drunkenly over the walls and the floor and the cheap plastic furniture. A dark lagoon oozed toward the door. And another long-legged body in an identical dress was bent over the bed, violently stuffing bits of gauze and tubes of lipstick into a shiny red bag shaped like a kissing mouth. The room smelled like artificial sweetener and old coins.

I slipped inside and kicked the door closed behind me. "Going somewhere?"

The girl spun to face me with eyes as wide as exit wounds. Black curls spilled around her face. A thin silver band wrapped around her throat, choker-style, with a teardrop pendant like a drop of blood between clavicles as deadly as a pair of freshly cut blades. The necklace.

Her painted mouth made a perfect O that somehow managed not to look practiced.

"I came to deliver a message from your sister." The mirror ball slowed to a stop. The dizzying lights from its reflection twisted sideways before it reversed and sent the room spinning again. "What happened here?"

Tears glittered in tracks through her makeup as if she was made of something purer than flesh and blood underneath the getup. She stuffed something else into her bag and kept her hand there. "I don't have a sister."

"That's funny." I inched toward the girl with my hands in the air. "I've got a 'gram with your face on it and a fat stack of holocred sitting in my bank account from someone who claims you have."

"We did the twin show." The girl's eyes flit to the corpse. Her knees trembled convincingly. "But she's not my sister. I just want to get out of here."

"Mama wants the drop." I took another half-step toward the girl with adrenaline kicking in the pit of my stomach. "That mean anything to you?"

The girl's expression didn't flicker. She was either really good, or really the wrong girl. The blank eyed stare of the corpse leered up at me. She had her own choker, a thin black line of seared flesh separating her head from her body.

The living girl twitched, and I looked up to see a little piss-kicker pointed at my guts. She said, "I'm leaving now."

Smoky black circles ringed her eyes with the kiss of glitter at the outer edges. Thick black eyelashes drooped seductively without her having to put in the effort. The silver dress slipped off a skinny shoulder. She licked her lips and smiled. The expression was as red as the kissy-faced handbag and just as empty. The silver choker danced in the reflection of the mirror ball. If you ignored the gun, she was the picture of a Saturday night good time. Hang onto your chips.

"That's a nice necklace." I kept my hands in the air and my voice steady.

Her free hand flew to her throat, and she narrowed her eyes, the thick lashes squeezing together like black teeth. "What's it worth to you?"

Blood hammered behind my eyes with the same insistent throbbing as the beat from downstairs. "Can you take it off?"

"That's what he wanted." She dropped her hand to reveal a clear droplet. Hadn't it been red before? The girl backed into the crumpled pile of bedding behind her. Her shoulders hunched, and she looked up at me with something wild clawing behind her eyes. "Slit her throat over costume jewellery."

The twin show. "Your friend had one too?"

"I was in the can." Faint bruises ran along the inside of the arm holding the gun. "I didn't see anything."

"Who was he?" I said. "Where did he go?"

"Ran off when I screamed." She tore the choker off and threw it on the body of the dead girl. "Take it. It's not worth another life. Not even one as cheap as all this."

Her pupils jumped to the necklace and then back to me. I could hear the gears grinding inside her head. Risk versus cush potential. Doing the math. The acrid scent of fear-sweat permeated the fake sweetness of powder and oils. Her skinny chest pumped like a rabbit's. I felt the barrel of the little hand cannon trained on me like a laser burning a hole in my stomach.

"I'm going to reach down and pick it up," I said. "Don't get excited."

Out in the hallway, LeRoy Lemieux's voice shouted something unintelligible. The girl flinched. I twisted to the side a millisecond before a crack loud enough to tear the fabric of the universe filled the room. The air on the left side of my body blistered. The shot hit the holopainted wall behind me and sent a spray of concrete gravel into the back of my head. She yelped and dropped her gun. They didn't call them pisskickers for nothing. She cradled her hand and glared up at me like I was the one who hadn't taught her how to shoot the damned thing.

I crouched to pick up the choker, keeping my eye on the girl. She bared her teeth at me and bent her knees, reaching down for the little gun. I knocked it under the bed. A blank, inhuman look flickered over her face. Then a feral scream ripped from her delicate throat. She clawed her way across the floor like she wanted to strangle me with her bare hands. Not fast enough. The cold metal of the necklace pooled like fresh water in my hand, and the empty pendant sat like a drop of water in the centre. Empty. Why did I think that? Her silver fingernails stabbed into my closed fist.

I grabbed her by the neck with the upgrade and lifted us both off the floor.

"What's the smoke, beautiful?"

She writhed in my grip like one of the glow-ups on the dancefloor, except she didn't look half so pleased with herself.

I said, "I'm not here to fight you."

She hissed through her teeth, words she wouldn't want her mother to hear. The thick crust of eyelashes on her left eye had peeled away from the lid and rested on my prosthetic like a fat caterpillar. Black and poisonous. The kind birds didn't eat. She dug her fingernails into my metallic wrist, and they tore away like chewed up silver leaves.

The door crashed open behind me and the girl boxed me in the groin with a stiletto shaped shoe. I threw her onto the bed and spun to face the party crasher. A dark shape stood in the doorway. I had expected the techRose goon, but against the electric blaze of black light on holopaint his silhouette was wrong. This was the lopsided triangle of a gym rat who spent too much time hitting the bench press and not enough time on his squats. Not the shapeless lump of Bug flesh.

The guy's face was dark and his feet were quick. A thin silver wire hung loosely between his gloved hands. He whipped it around in a well-oiled movement and snapped it tight. The silver glowed hot orange. LeRoy's body twitched in the hallway outside, the pylon suit muddy with a spray of blood. A black, sideways grin cracked the holopaint across the corridor. The perp must have been hiding in the room across the hall before he jumped LeRoy. The door now swung lazily open.

The girl leapt on my back and clawed at my real arm, trying to dig her way to the choker. She got a bony forearm around my throat. I gagged. The goon crept toward me. He had a shadow skin covering his face, but I could tell he was grinning. The bite of something sharp on my neck reminded me of the girl. I reached up and across my chest and hit her in the face with the hard goods. She dropped to the ground like a wet blanket.

"You shouldnta come here, baby." Shadow Skin had the voice of someone who loved his work a little too much. "Imma have to have a word with the boss man."

There was something about that voice. Downstairs the beat kicked it up a notch and sent the mirror ball jumping. The pale-rose spinners spiralled toward me like I was falling through stars. I shook my head. The reek of ozone sizzled from the thug's wire. He snapped it a couple times as he prowled toward me, just for effect. A twitch from the girl at my feet made my heart kick. The invisible grin on Shadow Skin seemed to widen.

The organ beat against my chest like it had had enough of this gig and wanted out of here. A black haze blurred out the edges of my vision. My head felt like I'd been hitting something harder than the pure stuff. The girl's silver dress seemed to spin at the centre of the room. The necklace slipped out of my fingers, and I reached up to touch the side of my throat. The little silver bee had stung me. My fingers buzzed and tingled.

The black haze became a flood and Shadow Skin went under the waves. My metal shoulder dragged on my body like a dead weight, and I felt the prosthetic fist spasming open and shut against my thigh. Systems down. The buzzing hit my face and my knees buckled.

I was out before I hit the floor.

CHAPTER 3

D ragging myself out of a drug-induced coma brought an ugly whiff of nostalgia with it. The back of my throat burned. My teeth had grown a skim of fuzz. I rolled over into a pool of my own vomit and groaned. No. This couldn't be.

Sickly pink fibres poked up out of the bilious mess like swamp grass. I gave everything I had to bring them into focus. Anxiety rippled through my body in a chilling wave, leaving goosebumps and electrified hairs in its wake. Where was I? How had I gotten there?

The burn of shame hit me so hard it obliterated everything else. Relapse. I hadn't had a drink in over a year. I'd hung up the habit when I turned in my badge. For good this time. I didn't know if I could face another Day One. I didn't even remember taking the plunge that drowned me this time. How could I let this happen again? The last thing I remembered drinking was the dirty glass of overpriced tap water and the leering weasel face of Sy the bartender.

Where?

TechRose. Red lights, spinning. Ripples of pink fabric against my face. The client's sister in a skimpy silver number with a drop of blood at her throat. The necklace.

My own neck ached like I'd lost a wrestling match with a python. I pushed myself off the ground with my metal arm. A lump under the prosthetic hand forced me to lean at an awkward angle, and a jolt of pain ran up my neck. I reached up with my flesh fingers and stroked the side of my throat. A welt raised up to meet me. My gaze slid back to the puddle of bile. The girl's pallid grey hand curled atop the hideous pink rug like a dead spider. The tip of the index finger sported a slick little number, a silver thimble with a stinger hanging off the end. Relief washed over me like a cleansing flood. Not a relapse.

With my soul washed clean of the insipient guilt, the relentless internal gaze turned outside again. My eyes travelled the length of the arm attached to the hand with the thimble. The girl was dead; the hole in her chest was about the right size to have been delivered by the pisskicker gripped in my metallic fist. She lay across her twin's body, both with the rigid posture of plastic dolls. They matched the plastic furniture of the room like toys discarded by a bored child. Tired playthings. The music downstairs throbbed, the mirror ball spun, the girls bled out their lives on the cheap, synthetic rug. The blood that hadn't been pumped out onto the carpet now pooled in black bruises along the underside of the bottom girl's legs. I reached out to touch the top girl's ankle. Cool but not yet cold.

I hadn't been out for long.

I pushed myself to my feet and scanned the room. No necklace. Shadow Skin had closed the door neatly behind him after tucking the girls in for the night. I looked at the gun in my hand and a wave of revulsion churned in my empty stomach. The nameless client. The girl with the necklace. Detective Thomas Weiland. The Shadow Skin. A gun in the hand that hadn't touched a gun since the accident.

It was a setup.

I stumbled over to the bed and grabbed the kissy-faced handbag off the rumpled covers, dumped the contents, and stuffed the gun inside. I didn't have time for a biosweep. Given the purpose of techRose's backrooms, the boys would have a hard time picking my signature out of the thousands of generous samples left behind by the customers, happy or not. The floor thrummed beneath my boots and the mirror ball spun ceaselessly, like Terra Firma corkscrewing its way around Sol. I slung the bag over my right shoulder, punched through the blackout curtains on the wall kitty corner to the bed, and knocked as much of the glass into the room as I could with my nerveless arm.

I pulled myself onto a rusted fire escape and into the rain. Of course it was raining. The sky above HoloCity never stopped pissing on us long enough for anyone to dry out. Below me, the grid hummed with blurs of light from private boilercars. A strand of wet hair the colour of well-chewed bubble gum fell in front of my face. I raked my fingers through my mop to slick it back and then pulled up the white synth-leather hood of my vest.

I didn't trust the grip of my real hand after whatever the girl had hit me with, but the upgraded seemed to rate. I swung myself over the railing and let myself drop to the next half-level, tucking the red bag under my arm like spoils from the world's saddest burglary. My shoulder wailed at me again—time to get it refit—and the fire escape swayed beneath my feet. When it held, I swung over once more and landed with a clang atop the big, green recycling bin behind techRose.

Some punters, even more desperate than the ones upstairs, had claimed the shadowed recesses between buildings in the alleyway for their transactions. The cha-ching of pro skirts collecting holocred by the minute echoed faintly through the hissing drizzle, but neither they nor their clients bothered to look up as I pelted past them through the puddles.

When I reached the grid, I found an empty yellow taxi ring to stand in while I brought up the slug schedule on my tattler. The ring would ding me a small stack of creds if I left without pickup, but at least it blocked the rain. That time of night, taxis were hard to come by. The other yellow rings lining the grid sheltered slumped figures who had the look of people who expected to die here, with dead eyes and their fare clutched in sweaty hands. The blue rings for personal pickup all stood empty—no one with money for personal boilers came down to the Grit District—so the pillars of light shone into the darkness as if their only purpose were to hold up the rain-laden sky.

The entrance to the underground and the nearest slug was a half hour away at any kind of pace I could keep up. The residue of the sleeper drug hung in my veins and each step felt heavier than the last. I shook my head again and peeked inside the bag. Still there. Not just a bad dream.

Another setup.

I had known the cops were trying to nail me even before Weiland's little visit. My career with the HoloCity PD had been a flash in the pan. A high-octane failure. I was nothing but a skid, a street kid, even when I passed my exams and slapped on the greys. I knew I'd been picked up to fill the Grit quota. I'd been the only one in my class. They had no choice. Back then, I couldn't stop drinking long enough to feel bad about it. They liked us Grits when they could get them. It's easy to buy off people who come from nothing. We do whatever we're told. Maybe if I'd been sober, I'd have been stupid enough to do just that.

Hopping from glow-up to hangover made it tough to remember what I was supposed to know and what I was supposed to forget. I forgot a lot of things, but never the right ones. Like that last bust. I got clever and remembered all kinds of things. I got so clever they accidentally assigned me a faulty plasma rifle and ordered me to spend all day firing it in the practice range. I was lucky the blast hadn't taken my head as well as my arm. The HoloCity PD wasn't.

But Lady Luck is like anyone else. She can be had for the right price. It was only a matter of time before Chief Swain paid up and I got knocked off. I didn't have enough chips in my corner to buy my own fate, but I could probably get myself out of town. I had enough cush and fake tickets to get down and stay down. The chief would forget about me. He'd managed to forget much more important things.

The chief. Shadow Skin must be one of his. But was he a cop or a grifter? I knew the voice. It floated around in my head like a mote of light. The memories of a drunk are ephemeral things. You can chase them, but every time you grab hold they show up outside your fingers. Only the ugly ones have enough substance to hang on to. You never catch the memories you want to keep.

On the grid, the boilers zipped by like streaks of neon in a cheesy strip joint, too fast and too bright to be real. I had just decided there was no chance of a cab when a yellow pod slowed and took the pickup track. If there were a couple more where it came from, I'd be gold. But when the pod passed up the first couple of yellow rings and headed for me, I wasn't feeling quite so shiny.

I cursed and backed out of the ring. My tattler chimed to let me know how much my stupidity was going to cost me, and I pounded it as far from the grid as I could get my jingle-brained ass

26

in a hurry. Of course they were monitoring the rings. Probably the slugs, too. But I might be able to afford a ScanAnon pass for the slug. Even if they tagged me, they couldn't swarm every station.

The pavement punched the soles of my boots and bit into my knees with every step, and I transferred the cred for a 24-hour ScanAnon transit ticket. The tattler gave a hollow chime, a and the ticket landed in my queue. That was it for my bank account. So much for getting out of town. I could get to my flat and grab the fake IDs, but I'd be pegging it out of HoloCity on my own steam now unless I could find somewhere local to scatter my signal.

I turned a sharp corner and skidded through a puddle. My feet slid out from under me. I caught myself on the upgrade and launched my body upright without skipping a step. What luck can't buy, practice can earn. Lucky for me, I had a lot of practice falling down. I landed in a Grit strip, teeming with the late-night crowd. The hockmarket.

HoloPops shouted from every corner, made bright in the rain, advertising goods and services from beyond the pale. A kaleidoscopic array of awnings sheltered the merrily misanthropic rejects of HoloCity. Hawkers and buyers, drunks and pinches. Stalls filled with disassembled electronics, illegal biotech, tanks with fleshy-bits floating in them. I hunkered under my white hood and forced my way into the crush of bodies. It would be slower going among the flood, but the exiles of polite society provided a temporary signal scatter better than my non-existent cred could buy.

By the time I dragged myself to the slug hole, the crowds had thinned. The amber light of dawn spilled through the haze of smog and rain like watered-down liquor. Belowground, blue-white tubes of florescence flickered off glossy fashion posters and the haggard faces of bar hoppers trying to live the dream. A homeless man slept on a piece of cardboard beneath a huge mural of two glittering bodies locked in a carnal embrace with the words "Big Bang" superimposed over it in holographic text. The letters flickered and became "Cosmo Relagé in the Stars."

I shook my head and slipped into the restroom inside the tube station. It was still illegal to have cameras in the can and HCPD more or less played by that rule. Hard-white lights flickered in the water-stained ceiling with a high-pitched whining that scratched inside my brain like a sharp-toothed parasite. I dug inside the biohazard receptacle with my metal arm, pushing aside needles and used feminine hygiene products, and ditched the handbag and the pisskicker inside. The bin hadn't been emptied in a few weeks and probably wouldn't be for a few more.

The best way to blend in in HoloCity is to stand out. I ducked into a stall and took my vest off. I shook the drops of rain off as best I could and turned it inside out so the fuzzy pink faux fox liner made my new skin. I stood in front of the mirror and applied a layer of red glitter to my lips. Just another go-go girl on the glow-down. I smudged the edges a little for effect. The old me stared out of the mirror with a sickly green complexion in the flickering light. Cheap habits and expensive lipstick. I punched the glass with my metal fist. My face shattered into a thousand fractals and broken pieces of me rained down on the tiles, tinkling like tears.

I pulled up the hood and ducked my face as I exited the throne room. They might not have eyes inside the can, but they watched those doors like peeping toms with their peckers out. I brought up the ScanAnon ticket on my tattler as I passed through the gate. My heart took a little vacation in my throat while we waited for the green light, but it rated. I licked my teeth at the HCPD uniform watching the queue. He looked right through me.

The ticket I rented my flat under was so flimsy a blind pincher could see through it, but it would hold for the early morning pencil pushers at HQ. I rode the slug an extra stop and hoofed it back to my block to be safe. I needed a little more abuse anyway. The sober life was making me soft. No way I'd have fallen for a setup like that when I was tuned up. I made a mental note to beat myself up again once my signal was good and scattered.

My building was one of those institutional grey numbers with little barred windows and about as much personality as a puddle of wet concrete. A red door—the architect's only conces-sion to festivity—had faded to puce and hung off its hinges like a tongue out of a hanged man's face. A pubescent beard of twisted grey shrubs sagged against the side of the building. It was just as nice inside as out.

In the early morning light, the rain pissed down in dingy golden sheets that would make a urologist wince. I ducked inside the back door and shuffled up the stairs as forlornly as possible. Too much pep in the step would attract the wrong kind of attention. On the third floor, I dragged my feet along a narrow corridor. The electric-blue indoor-outdoor carpeting was dimly illuminated by bare tubes overhead that seemed to buzz out as soon as I passed beneath them. Something small and black flitted through the shadows and squeaked at me angrily. Home sweet home.

I keyed in my code manually. The building had been built before tattlers took over for the part of our brains that had to remember passwords, ticket numbers, and ID signatures. Some nights, when I'd been too soused to access the flesh file, I'd slept out here with the buzzing lights and crawling carpets. That memory mote wasn't going anywhere. It was here to stay.

I slipped inside my flat and locked the door behind me. An undersized pig, fat and cartoonishly pink, blinked up at me from the living room floor. "What took you so long?"

"That's a new look." I dropped my vest on the threadbare arm of a lopsided armchair. The living room was furnished with thrift store rejects I had found collecting rainwater in some of HoloCity's finer hockmarkets. A dingy patchwork quilt of mismatched plastic planking made up the floor of the apartment. The planks came from filtered and recycled microplastics collected from Terra's rivers and oceans. Our landlord had gotten it cheap, because it turned out breathing in the gas and particulate from recycled microplastics is only marginally better for you than drinking them in your water. Even so, he hadn't bothered trying to find a matching set.

"You didn't seem to appreciate the cat module." The Smart-Pet spun in a tight circle and wagged its curly tail to show off the new skin. "Though I did have fun knocking things off tables."

One of my posters had come loose and dangled morosely off walls the colour and texture of crushed eggshells and coffee grounds. Remnants of my past life. The print 'grams had been ripped from the slug tunnels on drunken nights out. I can't remember exactly why any of them had appealed to me. I kept them up as a reminder that I'm not myself when I drink, and I really don't like the me who liked those trashy posters. A round, charging pad blinked in the far corner. It was just me and the SmartPet. I didn't even have a media screen to keep me company.

I reached down to pet the little pink piggy head and went into the kitchen to grab a can of NRG soda from the icebox. The SmartPet trotted after me. I took a swig of the poisonous energy drink and dug through the top drawer of the desk that doubled as my kitchen table. "Mittens was a holy terror."

"You could take off your boots, you know." The pig snuffled around my feet. "They've been contaminated by—"

"Listen, Miss Piggy. I need as much holocred as I can get, and fast. Is there anything we can sell?"

The pig mod rolled off toward the bedroom, its system making little clip-clop noises for its simulated hooves. It muttered, "You could stop giving so much of it to NRGCorp for one thing."

"One vice at a time, Piggler." The next drawer in my desk turned up a handful of credit chips, and I stuffed them into my pocket. "I need some IDs too. What have we got instant access to?"

"Would you settle on a name, please?" Beady brown eyes peered around the corner of my bedroom door. "It's difficult to establish an identity for this mod without a proper moniker."

"Baconator?"

"If you don't want my help, just say so." The pig huffed. "My battery is getting low. I'll go charge myself and maybe when that's done, you'll—"

"What do you have in mind, Princess Passive-Aggressive?"

"I like Hammett."

"Like the OE play?"

"That's Hamlet. I mean Dashiell Hammett. The Old Earth pulp-fiction writer." Hammett snorted. "I mean, you are a private investigator, and he practically invented—"

"I don't have time for a history lesson, Ham." I kicked the last drawer shut and started digging through the hall closet for a backpack. "I need a fresh falsie, holocred, and as many pairs of clean underwear as we can find. I've got to fade fast or I'm going to get faded out."

Hammett stamped a hoof. "You never listen to me."

"I know, I know." I picked up a pile of laundry off the bedroom floor, gave it a sniff, and stuffed it into the bag. "I was supposed to do the laundry on Wednesday."

"Wednesday three weeks ago." The pig wriggled under the bed and made a ping that made my heart sing. It wriggled out, pushing a blue credit chip with its little pink snout. "That's it for the apartment. And your false IDs are all stored at the office now."

I stood up into the top drawer of my wardrobe and collapsed on the ground with a welt on my head to match the one on my throat. The room swung around a few times to show me its good side and settled in slightly off kilter. "Whose bright idea was that?"

"Yours." Hammett dropped the blue chip in my lap proudly. "In fact, you insisted. In order to maintain a professional—"

"Mittens must have put me up to it." I rubbed my head. "Damn that cat."

Hammett rested its simulated chin on my thigh and blinked up at me with long-lashed brown eyes that were growing bigger by the minute. "How long will you be away?"

"Until it's safe to come home, Hammett."

"Is it that bad?"

"HCPD is trying to set me up for murder," I said. "You'd think it would be enough for me to be off the force, scraping the bottom of the barrel for private jobs. They could just wait for me to starve to death. Even Weiland is in on it now."

"Tom? He wouldn't—"

"He would," I said. "And he has. That man puts his career

before everything else. Even … whatever we were."

"Kind of like he said you did with—"

I slammed my hand into the wall. "I quit drinking, didn't I?"

Hammett jumped. "I know. I helped."

"You did more than help." I bent and scratched the pig between the ears. Hammett's big eyes closed appreciatively. "Maybe Tom needs a SmartPet too. The Workaholics Anonymous support chicken."

"Would you prefer a chicken?" Hammett cocked its head at me. "I can check the archives."

I laughed and let my hand drop. The pig nudged me with a cold, wet nose. Nice touch. I had to give the mod designers credit. It was a class skin. "How much did this cost me?"

Hammett's eyes swelled to the size of billiard balls. "I used a coupon."

"I need holocreds, Ham." I stood, narrowly avoiding the same mistake that had bought my last trip to the floor. "Is it returnable?"

"I returned Mittens." The pig's little triangle ears wilted comically. "I've been saving up. You really need them that badly?"

I pocketed the blue chip and did some mental bean counting. "You're going to be in maintenance for a while."

"That's okay." Hammett clip-clopped over to the SmartPet charging station in the living room with its curly pink tail drooping. "I've got updates to do."

I slung the silver backpack over my shoulder and bent to pat the pig's head one more time. "You sure there's a falsie at the office?"

"Two fresh ones and a handful of barely used," it replied and settled onto the charger. "Any final instructions?"

"Delete the transcriptions for this conversation." I tossed my NRG can into the recycling chute and tucked a pink jacket under my arm. "Maintenance mode. Free upgrades only. And if anyone other than me tries to bring you out of hibernation, wipe it all. Here and at the office."

The SmartPet nodded its piggy head and blinked at me one last time. "And Hammett?"

Return it. That's what I wanted to say. It might get me another few hops toward the edge of town. I couldn't get all the way outside HoloCity on the remaining ScanAnon hours. Scattering inside city limits would be expensive, too. Not to mention risky.

But the pig suited me better than any of the free mods we'd test driven since I shelled out for the thing with my first disability cheque. When I locked myself in the apartment, determined to dry out, the SmartPet kept me company and probably kept me sane. The pig skin was kind of cute. Plus, it looked so damned sad.

"Keep it." Hell. I was getting soft.

"Thank you!" Hammett stuck his nose in the air and grinned with Chiclet-white teeth no real pig ever sported.

"If I don't come back, it might get you a little better resale on the hockmarket," I said. "Besides, who else am I going to spoil?"

"Please be safe." The pig's eyes widened. "I've heard what happens to cheap sim units on the hockmarket, and I have no intention of becoming one of those sorts of companions."

"I'm sure they could fit you with the right holes and dongles." I opened the door to the murky blue corridor and gave my apartment a final farewell. "But I'll do my best."

I keyed in the code to lock the door. The faint electronic noises of the SmartPet powering down seeped through the thin walls and followed me down the hallway. A cheerful tune. I shuffled into the stairwell and the final notes lingered in my ears like a funeral dirge.

CHAPTER 4

I didn't have the stomach for another slug tube, so I hoofed it the extra few blocks to a SkyTrain station. It's not every day a girl scores the fast bird across town, and I only had about twenty hours left to use the ScanAnon ticket. I kept my jacket pink-side out and a bleary-eyed look on my face, but I cleaned up the red glitter a bit. Real down-and-out Grit skids only hit the fast bird stations to panhandle, and I didn't want to draw attention from security. The SkyTrains use private knuckle crackers instead of HCPD because they can afford it. They had enough cush to buy a lot of enthusiastic muscle.

I pulled a pair of opalescent visilens shades over my eyes and did a quick visual scan of my empty accounts as I filed up the corrugated metal staircase up to the bird. Hammett had been right. Even the secondary accounts were emptier than the hooch shop shelves on benefits day. I had nothing but the chips in my pocket. Maybe I had a few cred stashed away at the office with my falsies. That would be luckier than I had any reasonable hope to expect.

The shades bought me just enough credibility in the early morning SkyTrain crowd for security to pass me over. I scanned my ticket and jumped the first bird downtown in a matter of twenty minutes. The rain even decided to take a breather though a vortex of sludgy grey clouds that whirled over HoloCity like the eye of God waiting to drown us for our sins. Sometimes I wondered if the weather system was manufactured for the sole purpose of making HoloPops more effective, rain being a much cheaper surface to project on than nanoparticles.

The western edge of the city disappeared into the flat grey mist of the optimistically dubbed Sapphire Sea, where the first bangtail shuttles launched their way through the swirling clouds, the orange-gold glow of their boosters streaking upward like the tails of impotent firecrackers. I watched them anyway. Someday, one might burst in a climactic eruption of elitist wealth and rain flaming holocred chips on the city below. That would be a sight.

When none of the bangtails exploded, I spun around to look out my own window. Riding the fast bird was a private pleasure. The view was completely unlike anything a Grit skid like me should ever get to see. I was a stranger to my own city up here, removed from the synthetic cesspool of street life. A silent observer soaring just below the clouds. The light of Sol burst through the cumulonimbus in violent spears of orange light, illuminating patches on buildings like beams from a plasma rifle. Target engaged. Bang.

Only one building seemed immune. The Mezzanine Rose, a sprawling expanse of glittering pink and white glass, glowed as if with an internal light of its own to neutralize the wrath of Sol. It spiralled out from the centre in a bloom of fractals like an architectural wet dream. Inside those shimmering walls was perhaps the only respite from the techno vomit spewed across the rest of the city. No biotech, no cyber enhancement, no net access, and no inorganic intelligence was allowed within its walls.

They called themselves the Last Humanist Church and the pink-robed acolytes followed the Four Absolutes: Absolute Honesty, Absolute Purity, Absolute Unselfishness, and Absolute Love. It's the Absolute Purity angle that made them odd ducks in HoloCity. Purity to the Last Humanists had nothing to do with sex, but Purity of body, mind, and soul in the face of what they saw as the cybernetic threat to humanity. Powerful freedom of expression laws protected the Mezzanine Rose from literal and virtual contamination. Within the church, the human being in its purest form still reigned. The idea held some appeal. Maybe some day I'd ditch my upgrade, get a nanoparticle flush, and become a pink-robed acolyte in my retirement.

I was still laughing at the idea when I slammed open the door to my office and made Dickie Roh fall out of my chair. He peered up at me from the floor with a magnifying glass pressed up against his eye. He winked at me like a lopsided cyclops. "Hey, Bubs, what's the smoke?"

"Get off the floor, Dickie." I tossed my jacket and back on the chair he'd just evacuated. "I need you to dig up a fresh falsie for me and whatever cred we have laying around. I need to get out of town for a while."

Dickie picked himself up, but he turned his magnified eye on me and adjusted the ridiculous Homburg hat perched precariously on his head. "You didn't just say that."

"The old-fashioned Private Eye thing is cute, Dick." I pushed the chair back and got on my hands and knees underneath the desk, groping around for any chips that might have rolled underneath the furniture when I was feeling too flush to chase after them. "But I'm serious. I need a vacation, or I'm going to be retired permanently."

"I'll have to change the sign on the door." He turned his big brown blinker to the frosted glass etching that proclaimed the dingy room to be the office of BUBBLES MARLOWE: PRIVATE INVESTIGATOR. I still had trouble supressing juvenile giggles over that one, but Dickie was dead serious about our racket. "And the business cards."

"What are you on about?" I tossed a pen at him and knocked the Homburg off his slicked-back black hair. "I don't even have business cards."

"BUBBLES MARLOWE: PSYCHIC DETECTIVE." He waved a hand

over the glass as if magically conjuring a new sign. "It does have marketing potential."

My secretary was endlessly enthusiastic to expand his tattler and email handling repertoire into other realms. Interior design. Marketing and promotions. Assistant P.I. He wanted to do it all so badly I didn't even have to pay him. Good thing, too, because I couldn't afford to. Dickie comes from money. His parental units run a wildly successful PornoPop franchise out of the HoloCity Biz District. Big money. I met Dickie when I busted up a gang of petty thieves who thought they'd hit the big time with a quick and easy kidnapping scheme. Trouble is, Dickie's parents hadn't realized he was missing yet, and the thieves were too small time to get themselves noticed. He'd been hanging upside down in a makeshift cell for a week when I found him. I've always wondered if all the extra blood flow to his brain sent him over the edge. Anyway, he never did go home after that. He hung around the station for a while, trying to get my number, and when I got canned, there he was with a business proposal. And a personal allowance.

"Dickie, have you been day drinking?"

Dickie dropped the magnifying glass on the desk and picked the gunmetal grey Homburg off the floor. He wiped off some imaginary dirt and hung it on the coat rack. His lips pulled down into a sad clown frown. "Funny you should ask. I was just wondering the same thing about you."

"I've had a rough night." I stood up and cracked my head on

the desk for good measure. Cursing, I fell back into the chair and crushed the backpack. I tugged it out from under my ass, tossed it on the floor. "But I'm sober. If this keeps up, though, I'm going to reconsider my life choices."

"You look like last night's dinner splattered on the transport grid."

I checked my skull for soft spots. "I bet you say that to all the ladies."

"When did you enter the Lucky Bastard Sweepstakes?" Dickie opened the little office cooler and tossed me an NRG can.

"Exactly never." I iced goose-egg number three and started rifling through drawers. "Are you going to help me or not?"

"I'm no Private Eye," Dickie said, kicking the fridge closed and cracking open his own can, his voice a little wistful as if to say *some day* … "But I'm pretty sure you have to enter to win."

"The only thing I've ever won is an early retirement." I found a piece of stale gum along with a ten-spot chip tucked in the back of the filing cabinet. I shoved the gum into my mouth. "And I had to blow off my arm to do that."

"Well then, consider yourself a Lucky Bastard." Dickie punched a button on the wall and a HoloPop of the new luxury cruise satellite ship *Island Dreamer* spun in the middle of the room. Beneath the behemoth space craft neon block letters screamed CONGRATULATIONS! BETTY MARLOWE, YOU ARE A WINNER!

"When did you get this?"

"*You* received the notification shortly after you left for your stakeout last night." He punched the button again, and the HoloPop disappeared. "I tried to ring your tattler, but you've got comms blocked. Again."

I checked my settings. He was right. I flicked on comms and notifications again and was assaulted by a barrage of tuneless pinging. Wincing, I opened my energy drink and took a swig. "Sorry. You didn't sleep here all night, did you?"

Dickie rubbed a faintly stubbled chin. "Well. I didn't sleep that much."

Most of the pings were the usual ads and garbage, but I did have a missed call from my client at about the time Weiland was wagging his gums at me. I hit the recall and leaned back in my chair.

"Marlowe? Oh … I'm sorry. I hope this message reaches you in time." The client's breathless voice whispered through the office speakers. Like the last time we spoke, it was filtered through a tone scrambler so that she sounded like many people speaking at once. "The job I hired you for … everything's going sideways. I have reason to believe my sister is already … Look, I'm sorry to have wasted your time. Do not attempt to contact her. It may be too dangerous. I'm sorry."

"It was that bad?"

"Worse," I said, showing him the welt on my neck. "The

43

girl was dead when I got there, and another one got me with a ring-stinger before her insides got shown the way out."

Dickie crushed his can and popped it into the recycling chute. He tipped his head at the tattler. "At least she's sorry."

"It was a setup." I balled my can up into a tight sphere with the upgrade and made a shot for the chute.

The can fell short, but Dickie dove for it and smacked it with the palm of his hand just far enough for the vac seal to open up and suck it home. He did a victory lap of the office with his hands raised about his head, hissing the sound of distant applause. "And the crowd goes wild!"

"Sit your ass in a chair, Dick." I dug the pitiful collection of cred out of my pockets and stacked them on the desk. "This is serious."

Dickie plunked into a silver task chair and spun around to face me. "How much do you need?"

"I've got a whopping seventy-eight cred to my name right now," I said. "And with that last gig busting out, it's not getting better any time soon. There must be something around here we can sell. You can transfer the cred to my account. I've got to move before the time runs out on my transit pass."

Dickie brought up a holoscreen from the other side of the desk and started flipping through files. "Is a 500 spot enough?"

"We don't have anything worth that much." I looked around the office, bare except for the shared desk, a couple of chairs, the coatrack, and the mini-fridge. Minimalist Chic, according to Dickie. Looked more like Poor Man's Industrial to me. "Can you live without the cooler for a couple of—"

My tattler pinged a notification. A stack of five hundred cred landed in my main account. "Dickie, you can't—"

"I didn't." His eyes folded into gleeful crescent moons above his round cheeks as he grinned through the holoscreen at me. "That was your apologetic benefactor."

"Her sister was dead before I could deliver the message." I flipped through the statement screen. No notes. Just the client code. And a fat stack of cred. "I can't accept this."

"Maybe it wasn't a setup," Dickie said.

"I know a steaming pile when I smell it, Dick." I ran my fingers through my hair and pulled hard enough to make my eyes water. "I don't have time to sit here and puzzle it out. I have to scatter. The chief is out for blood this time."

"You think Swain is behind it?" Dickie's cheeks dropped and his brown eyes widened. Then he clapped his hands together so hard I felt it in my teeth. "Excellent!"

I glared and kicked him in the shin under the desk. He yelped and spun into the middle of the room.

"I didn't will the agency to you," I said. "So don't order the cake and holostreamers just yet."

"HoloCity PD has no jurisdiction—" A thought dawned on him like a poke in the eye. He squinted at me. "Wait, who did you will it to?"

"Focus, Dickie." I stood, stuffed the measly pile of credit chips back into my pocket, and grabbed my backpack off the floor. "The goal is for me *not* to get faded by Chief Swain's goons."

"Why scatter in the suburban slums when you can drift away on an *Island Dream*," Dickie said, grinning again. He kicked himself over to the wall and hit the button again. A massive ship with *Island Dreamer* plastered across its hull in crisp white lettering hovered in the middle of the office with CONGRATULATIONS! blinking underneath it.

"A vacation." The pieces started to click together like hungry teeth. "And HCPD—"

"Can't touch you." Dickie did another victory lap around the office. "They don't have jurisdiction outside the stratosphere directly above HoloCity limits, or in any station associated with international space travel."

"You checked it out?" I ask. "This thing's legit?"

"Boarding started three days ago," he said. "Today's the last day to catch a public bangtail. Tomorrow the private shuttles will dock and then—" He made a soaring motion with his hands.

"Seems too good to be true."

"You'll probably have to fend off an army of timeshare pushers." His shuttle crashed and burned into an open palm. "And your room is going to be full of Lucky Bastard gin. But ..."

"Gift horses," I said. "Got it. What time is the next shuttle?"

"There's a nooner and a four o'clock." He picked up his Homburg and placed it delicately atop his slicked-back 'do. "Enjoy the vay-cay. I'll hold down the fort."

"Thanks, Dickie. You're a peach." I snagged another can of NRG. "Don't sign for any packages with my name on them. No telling when Swain's going to try to blow off another chunk of me."

I flung open the door and crashed directly into a tall, black-skinned woman who cracked me in the face with a long metal case the size of a plasma rifle.

"You're not going anywhere, Bubbles." She pinned me to the wall with a steely eyed stare from behind huge, thick-rimmed glasses. "I've got a little gift for you."

CHAPTER 5

"What are you doing here, Rae?" I rubbed the bridge of my nose "I didn't order a nose job."

"I have something else for you." She squeezed between me and the door frame and squinted her eyes at my swelling sniffer. "Sorry about your face. Though it might be an improvement. Are you going for washed up hooker or poorly maintained sex-doll?"

"Either will do if it earns me an ounce of invisibility where the cops are concerned." I shoved her into the room and closed the door again.

Rae Adesina blinked big black eyes at me. She had electric-blue eyeliner drawn all the way into her hairline. "I do like the lipstick. Is that a Cosmo colour?"

"Blood of my Enemies."

Rae grinned. "I knew it. I have been a good influence on you after all."

"Not good enough," Dickie piped up from behind me. "Apparently."

Rae's blue eyeliner matched her impeccably teased afro, which had been sculpted into a long, egg-shaped protuberance from the back of her skull. On anyone else it would have looked like an aborted alien fetus, but somehow, combined with her height and the intensity of her eyes, the outlandishness of her coif added to the gravitas of her appearance. Below her face, she donned a simple white lab coat and a sensible pantsuit of an equally shocking blue. "What did you do this time?"

"It's less what I did and more what I didn't do." I folded my arms and watched her cross the room and set the metal box on my desk with a clang. "And what a certain Chief of Police would like to do to me."

She flipped open the lid to reveal a layer of protective foam padding. "They still giving you the shake down over that drug bust that wasn't?"

Dickie spun slowly on his chair without taking his eyes off the Cerulean queen with his gob smacked into next week.

"All I know is someone went to a lot of trouble to make me look like a half-rate hitman, and it has Stench-O-Swain dripping out of every orifice."

"Lovely visual, thank you for that," she muttered over the box.

Dickie's chair had spun to face the wall, and he craned his neck and contorted himself like a dancer with the rent due to keep his eye on the prize. "What's in the box, Rae?"

"Before I show you"—Rae whirled on me, ignoring Dickie completely—"I want a promise."

"There is a literal time bomb with my name on it ticking in my tattler right now, Rae. I had two opportunities to get out of town, and you've blown the first one. So say what you think you need to say and let me get out of here. My promises are worth about as much as a pinch's piss. I've got a price on my head. Even if I smile and nod, I can't make good on it when I'm dead."

"It's about Jimi."

I rolled my eyes to the ceiling and said a silent prayer to the Last Humanist Church of the Mezzanine Rose. Why not. I'd tried all the other deities over the years, and they'd gotten me into this hole. "I told you about Jimi. There were drugs in his system. You saw what happened to me the last time I asked questions about a drug case. There won't be anything left of me for you to put back together if I ask about another one; I'm not a uniform anymore. Jimi Ng's case is closed as far as HCPD are concerned. If I start digging into it, Chief Swain is going to send the circus after me."

"He's already after you." Rae's broad mouth flattened into a thin line, and she hit me with a hard stare. A nerve in my shoulder gave me a twinge for good measure. "Even he can't kill you

51

twice."

"He can probably take twice as long doing it, though. That's what scares me."

"When was the last time your upgrade was refitted?" She cocked her head at me, and with the alien mane attached to the back of her head, the effect was slightly predatory. "Your left arm is hanging about and inch lower than it should."

I groaned. I dropped the backpack, whipped off my jacket, and stood reluctantly in front of her, trying to prepare myself for the tirade. "It hurts a bit."

"Of all the jingle-brained—" Rae interrupted herself with a sigh like opening the floodgates on a raging river. She closed her blue-lined eyes and counted silently under her breath. "Bubbles, you have to take care of yourself. Proper equipment maintenance is essential to your health, like getting enough sleep, drinking filtered water, and eating vegetables."

"Vegetables are too expensive, I can't remember the last time I slept, and the last glass of water I drank cost me a hundred cred and came straight from the tap at techRose."

"If you treat your body like a black-market dumpster—" She turned around and peeled off the layer of protective foam. "—some day you'll end up in one."

"The circle of life." Dickie grinned. "You should be glad she hasn't ripped the arm off and sold it by now."

"Think I'd get anything for it?"

Something shiny glinted from inside the box and Dickie's eyes went wide. His jaw scraped the floor. He shook his head at me. "Play nice with the lady, Bubbles. She brought you a hell of a present."

Rae picked up the thing in the box and turned to face me. A new cybernetic prosthesis, long and slender and looking more like an arm than an exoskeleton, lay across her arms like an offering. "If this attachment shows up on the hockmarket, my job will be forfeit."

I made a low whistle. "Who did you have to kill to steal that thing?"

Rae shook her head and tapped a stilettoed toe impatiently. "It's a prototype. And I didn't steal it, I have it signed out for field testing."

"Looks like it's made out of well-chewed bubble gum," Dickie said. "Bet you have to pay extra for the pink model."

Rae said, "You can change it in the options menu."

The arm had a pearly sheen to it and almost perfectly matched the colour of my hair. "Going for the hard sell."

"Take off your shirt and I'll get you fitted." Rae's bedside manner voice kicked in. "Dickie, help her get the old one off and place it in the box for me."

Dickie hopped to like a well-trained soldier and held onto my metal arm while I shrugged out of my thin white t-shirt. He winked at Rae. "Who says I'm not getting paid?"

I swung the arm into his gut and listened with satisfaction to the rush of air that escaped his lungs. "For old time's sake."

I loosened the fasteners and twisted out of the attachment. It released with a sucking sound and the sour metallic smell of sweat and titanium. Dickie wrinkled his nose and shuffled over to the box on the desk, still slightly bent over and gasping. I avoided looking at my bare shoulder where the stump of bone was covered with a gnarled mass of scar tissue like red tree-bark.

He brought a container of talc from the box and dusted the damp flesh. "You're a little ripe under there. When's the last time you took that thing off?"

My muscles twitched to send the arm into his stomach again. My phantom arm swung, but nothing happened. He grinned.

"That's enough," Rae said and approached with the new arm. "It's going to take some time to get everything connected properly. I want you to listen to me—"

"The arm rates, Rae, it really does. But I can't help you with Jimi. We've been over this before. Weiland and I nailed a low-level pusher with those vials, but the bust went bad. The buyer got away, and the vials ended up being a hoax. Chief Swain made it very clear we'd made some very important people very angry."

"And within twenty-four hours Jimi was very dead from a drug overdose along with about three hundred other people." Rae slipped the arm on gently but she spoke through gritted teeth.

"Whip Tesla, the pusher, was out on the streets before the

end of our shift. We knew it stunk. Weiland shut up and wagged his tail like a good little doggy. When the body count started climbing, I nosed around a bit and got my arm blown off for the trouble."

"Jimi didn't use drugs." Rae wrenched a little harder on the arm than she needs to. A nerve shock spasmed through the metallic pink fingers. "He was a brilliant scientist. I loved him but I wasn't blind."

"There were plenty of people who would have sworn I wasn't a drunk." I rolled my shoulder to test the fit. The joint was so smooth it made my real ones feel like rusty old machinery. "I'm sorry he died. I liked Jimi. But sometimes our numbers get called before our time. There doesn't have to be a reason for it."

"Jimi's death wasn't some tragic mistake or a goddamned coincidence, Bubbles." Rae dropped the doctor act and punched me in the chest with both fists. Tears threatened her carefully applied makeup, glittering like diamonds around her coal-black irises. "He was onto something big. I need to know why he was killed. I need you to help me."

I flexed the new fingers. "Dickie, get me a mirror, would you?"

Dickie stood, frozen. He watched us with a strange, blank look on his face.

"Dickie?"

"Sorry." He shook his head and punched a button on the

wall, and I stared into the eyes of a hologram of myself. They were right; I did look like death warmed over. I twisted to see the upgrade from all angles. My stomach muscles bunched underneath the pinched folds of skin where a synthetic plate held in the guts on the left side of my body.

When I went down, HoloCity General wrote me off for parts. I didn't have friends in high enough places to deserve the surgery necessary to put Humpty Dumpty back together again. Rae paid the premium to get me while I was still fresh and signed my body out under an assumed name. She did the work to put me back together herself. Money can't buy that kind of service. When it comes down to it, friends in low places always rated higher than cush from on high. There wasn't much difference between Rae's work and a pro job, unless some pencil pusher looked real close at the enhancement tickets.

"This is class equipment, Rae." I pulled my shirt back on and shrugged on my jacket. "And it's pink."

Rae crossed her arms over her chest and raised her finely sculpted eyebrows at me. "And?"

Maybe I was just another project to her. Maybe she'd needed something to keep her mind off Jimi when the wound was still raw. Whatever the reason, the fact was that she brought me back from the dead. It might cost me my life to help her, but I owed it to her anyway. My resolve evaporated like fumes off a boiler car on a cold night.

"And I'll see what I can dig up about Jimi." I sighed. Twice in one day. I was definitely getting soft.

"Thank you, Bubbles." Rae wrapped me in her long arms and squeezed until I saw stars dancing. "I knew I could count on you."

"When in doubt, put your money on the pony with three legs and nothing but pride to lose."

She released me and stood back, wiping her eyes. The blue paint stayed exactly where it was supposed to. Witchcraft. It was the only explanation.

"I've got to drift now, seriously." I picked my bag back up off the floor. "If I don't catch the four o'clock bangtail, you'll have to go morgue diving to get your prototype back."

"Bangtail?" Rae put her hands on her hips. "I haven't even shown you how to use all the features yet. Where the hell—"

The office tattler pinged and a fuzzy 'gram of Chief Swain's face hovered in the middle of the room with his jaw muscles flexing as he chewed up the words he was going to spit in my direction if I was stupid enough to take the call. I was. Maybe I was feeling a bit masochistic.

"Swain." I grinned at him. "It's so nice of you to call!"

He glowered at me over the 'gram. "I warned you, Marlowe. Stay off my turf. Next time I catch you sniffing around where you don't belong—"

"You'll what? Take my other arm? Maybe you'll get it right and kill me properly."

"I'm not going to kill you, girl." Swain sneered at me with crooked yellow teeth and a cruel look twisting the flesh around his eyes. "Death would be too easy. I'm going to take everything from you. Your friends. One by one. Your business. Your sobriety... Then I'm going to watch while you kill yourself—"

The 'gram blinked off and Rae stood next to the desk, her hand on the comms button. She said, "That's about enough of that."

"Thanks, Rae." I swallowed against the thick feeling in my throat and headed for the door.

Dickie stared at the place the hologram had been. "I really hate that guy."

"Understatement of the year." I yanked the door open and swung into the hall. "Fill her in, Dick."

I expected Dickie to jump on the double entendre, but he stood with his arms at his sides and watched me go.

"Don't take any more calls from the goons in grey." I reminded him. "The scatter starts now."

Rae's voice followed me into the hall, carrying the sharp edge of warning. "Bubbles, if you lose that arm in space I will kill you myself."

CHAPTER 6

I hopped a slug to Harbour Station and double checked that the five hundred spot still sat in my bankroll. Why would she pay me for a job I didn't do? The transaction lounged there like a fat house cat lording over the feral scraps of my usual contracts. Under normal circumstances I wouldn't touch the ephemeral cush, expecting it to fly out of my account as unexpectedly as it appeared. But I was going to need it. I may have won passage on the *Island Dreamer,* but life aboard a luxury cruiser wasn't going to come cheap and I had to be able to blend in. Looking like a washed up pro skirt wasn't going to cut it in the bangtail queue. I needed a class look and fast.

I browsed the shops along the Harbour Station strip on my visilens screens as the slug hummed through the underground tunnels. HoloPops screamed for my attention through the windows on the train, but the mag tracks made for a smooth ride. Most slugs I'd ridden tried to rattle you apart before you reached your destination. I guessed even the kind of clientele that deigned to take a train to the bangtails warranted the silk ride. Nice to live the cush life.

Most of the shops I pinged were way out of my league, but I found a second hand boutique with a virtual fitting room and sifted through their selection with the silence of the slug stuffing my ears like cotton. A couple of pieces looked good enough to get me on board the *Dream* but wouldn't blow through the dough before I had a chance to figure out the long-run cost of a scatter in the exosphere. I put them on hold and flipped up the opalescent lenses to scan my fellow slug riders.

An old couple sat across the slug car from me, so close to one another it looked like they'd decided to save some money and share the same plastic hip. A small, practical suitcase marshalled out front of their primly squared toes. They each had a wizened grip on the handle in order to ward off thieves who might be interested in outdated tech and neatly folded clothes that smelled faintly of butterscotch and mothballs.

Next to them, co-eds dressed like high-fashion pro skirts giggled and flashed the latest in tattler upgrades at one another, posing for selfies and vlogging the experience of slumming it on the slugs. A fog of high-cush perfume—Queen of Hearts by Lorena Valentia—oozed out of their greasepaint stuffed pores. I gritted my teeth and turned my gaze to the front of the car. Even I knew that Cosmo Cosmetics had done it first and done it better with their Queen of Tarts line, and I couldn't afford either. These fashionista numbskulls would never be able to tell the difference between vogue and vulgar unless it came with an identifying price tag. Valentia, in a typical Biz District move, mined the Grit for trends, made a pale copy of "edgy" street styles, and then charged five times the cred for comfort couture. That's highbinder class for you.

At the front of the car, the dusty-rose robes of New Humanist acolytes stacked against each other like dominoes, filling two rows on both sides at the front of the slug. Fashion was something the members of the church didn't bother themselves with too much. Uniform conformity to highlight the divine individuality of the human form or something like that. What were they doing on their way to the bangtail station?

The back was empty except for a Grit District bum who'd fallen asleep underneath one of the benches and missed his stop. Harbour Strip security would nab that one and give him a work-over he probably wouldn't remember. He slept with one eye cracked open and pointed at me. I watched for a while, but he didn't blink. Dead, maybe. Or maybe it was that tainted euphoric that had hit the streets shortly after we were forced to let Whip Tesla out on the long leash with nothing but faith that Chief Swain had ever seen the other end of it. Tropical Punch. Sometimes it gave the pinches a nice glow-up, and sometimes it blew open all their neural pathways and left them frozen in nightmares inside their own heads until their hearts forgot to keep beating. What a way to go, Jimi Ng.

I pulled down my glasses, put some white noise in the ear tubes, and let my head fall back. The lack of sleep hit back like the floor after thirteen ruby gimlets at techRose. Hard and fast. I woke when the slug slowed for Harbour Station with a crick in my neck and a damp patch on my neck where I had been drooling. I killed the white noise and nestled my glasses into my hair. The co-eds tittered across the aisle, but I refused to turn around in case it was me they were vlogging now. The last thing I needed was to go viral for beating up a younger, cuter woman with a million cred wadded up in her—

"Oh my Holy Origins," one of them fake whispered to the others. "Are you getting this? Total system failure."

"Where does an off-grid like that even find the juice to nerve fry?" One snapped her gum. "Getting punched is cushy. Remember when—"

A barrage of pings from their tattlers sent them into another fit of giggles as the slug slid to a stop and the doors slid open. "OMHO, are you live feeding, you vetch?"

The squad bounced out of the car in a pink cloud of candy-scented synthetics. The elderly couple stood as one, bent over the suitcase like twin lampposts, and shuffled after the gigglers. Behind me, the acolytes filed out of the front doors, silent as a grid failure. The homeless man struggled to his feet and dragged himself toward the exit with his legs lurching like dead weights from his hips. One glazed eye remained trained on me. I wondered if he had taken a punch from a cut batch of the new drug. He wouldn't be the last.

I took the front door and left him floundering. Harbour Station security would take care of him, one way or another. I stepped directly into the path of the acolytes, who came at me like moths to a neon light. Had they been waiting for me? They stared at me with mask like expressions of neutrality.

One of them smiled like a HoloPop salesman. "Greetings, traveller. Are you embarking on a journey?"

"Sorry," I said, trying to move past them. "I don't have time for the Purity chat right now."

They moved around me like a pink cloud, filling in the spaces between them before I could move. The smiling one said, "The human body is an incredible thing. It's a shame to see it adulterated so."

"It was a plasma rifle that adulterated my body." I pushed the smiling one out of my way. "If my prosthesis offends you, you can stop staring at it."

They all smiled suddenly, with eerie benignity. In unison, they said, "Have a nice trip."

I broke free of the acolytes and shook off a chill. Must be a cult. They're all brainwashed lunatics. I blinked up at the glare of overcast skies above. This was the only slug station that let out on the surface. HS security personnel were scattered like black confetti across the harbour, and a handful of grey HCPD uniforms livened up the mix. I let my eyes float over them with calculated indifference as I scanned the strip for Hack Seconds. I pulled my hood up and jogged across the commons toward the neon haze of its windows glowing through the rain. Of course it was raining again.

At the end of the strip, the sea churned like my stomach after a bender. The only thing blue about the Sapphire Sea was the chunks of plastic floating on the surface like bits of indigestible trash in dog sick. The queues for the four o'clock bangtails already stretched out of the designated area, and late-comers were getting the water treatment on the uncovered imitation cobblestones outside the station. I left them there and ducked into the secondhand shop.

Behind the counter of Hack Seconds, the salesboy glanced up from a PornoPop holorag. He hastily flipped it closed and came around the side with his best attempt at the customer-service smile. "Welcome to Hack Seconds where you'll find designer brands, rate seconds, and—"

A doll-like contortionist let out a wet groan from the counter top where the rag had fallen open again. The service boy leaped for it with his face the colour of boiled lobster chips.

I hit him with a glare of schoolmarm severity and pointed to the stack of clothes he'd folded and set aside for me. "Where's the change room?"

"Back here." He grabbed a key fob from underneath the

counter where the holorag now had a box of tube upgrades sitting on top of it. "Sorry about that."

"Don't let yourself get any funny ideas about the natural range of human flexibility and we'll call it even."

"Sure." The lobster chips looked a little burnt. He opened the door for me. "I know that."

I stepped inside and stripped out of my Gritwear. I tugged on a shiny white jumper that had star-cruise socialite written all over it. It was hideous and it suited me perfectly. The halter neck left my upgrade free to move and showed off enough of the goods to distract all but the most dedicated, het-oriented, male officers of the law. I stuffed my jacket and street clothes into the shiny silver backpack. It was so old, I figured I could get away with it as a retro style piece. My boots made an aggressive, post-futurist statement against the glam white suit. I used the mirror to tousle my pink hair the way I'd seen a couple of the co-eds do it and applied red glitter in clean lines to my lips and eyes. I didn't have Rae Adesina's gravitas, but I made up for it with my own secret weapon: an implication of high-cush moral flexibility. I pinged the sale through and stuffed the purchases into the bag too.

The salesboy's larynx bobbed a couple times when I stepped out of the change room. I grabbed a clear umbrella with an opalescent sheen to it as I walked through the door and trusted him to charge it to the same bill once his wires uncrossed. The new look had the effect I was going for. Before the door had swung closed behind me, the holorag was panting again. Maybe the umbrella would be on the house.

I tested my strut across the commons, putting as much sway into each step as I could without letting gravity win the battle against my top half. It had been a while since I'd worked any kind of juice, and I felt like a damned glam-poppet. But harbour security guards followed my movements with appreciative eyes and kept a respectful distance. There seemed to be more of the black smudges looming out of the rain, but maybe that was just me being a bit tight. Don't second guess it, I told myself. Looking like you want to be noticed is the best way to avoid getting the kind of attention that has the black eye of a gun barrel attached to it. I eyed the queues and tried to figure which one was for "lucky winners." I didn't want to blow my cover by hopping the wrong line and causing a scene when the outfit says I know what I'm doing.

Acolytes of the Last Humanist Church seemed to deserve their own jump point. A thin file of damp, pink robes shuffled inside the station—many more than had been riding the slug with me. The segregation made sense enough; they wouldn't want to expose their wholesome flesh to the nanoparticles and radio waves or whatever else they thought the rest of us were oozing into the atmosphere with our unbridled desire to foul the natural purity of our human forms. But why was the Last Humanist Church sending its purest disciples to the *Island Dreamer* at all? Probably there to convert the lowly technofilth when they're on the glow-down and hit the holowall of despair.

A commotion at the slug pulled some attention away from me. I flipped down my glasses and flicked on the mirror lenses so I could watch while maintaining an air of self-absorbed indifference. The Grit scrub leaned on one of the officers, waving one arm wildly, his dead, flat eye still trained on me like one of those analog paintings in a retro-grade museum that seemed to follow you as you moved about the gallery.

An uncomfortable thought dawned on me, and I hustled my swagger toward the tail end of the shortest queue. I pulled up behind a couple techrotic bros with enough black-market gear to drain a micro trade zone's cush roll. One eyed me obliquely with a mechanical iris and nudged his buddy with all the subtlety of a gearhead on the glow-up. A shout exploded from the scuffle of security manning the slug trail.

"Mind if I jump the line, baby?" I placed my upgrade on Bug-Eye's shoulder. "The views even better from that angle."

"I don't know." His pal grinned at me with metal teeth. "It's looking pretty good right now. What's in it for us?"

Feet pounded through puddles across the commons toward me. I watched them in my mirrors but didn't turn my head. "A smooth ride or a whole lot of pain. You decide."

"Skip it, bro." Bug-Eye started to turn again. "There's vetch aplenty onboard the *Dream* fresher than this piece."

An HS security office put up his hand to accept a transmission. His mouth formed the words, "We've got her."

"Time's up, sugar cube." I punched through Bug-Eye's back plate with my upgrade and whipped him backwards. The new hydraulics had a bit more kick than my old arm, and he flew through the air like a metal rag doll, crashing into the first wave of HS goons with the satisfying crunch of hardware failure. I turned to his pal. "I had hoped you'd pick the pain train."

The techhead swung at me with an arm like a sledgehammer. But like most bros, he was all show and no go. I punched him in the flesh under the attachment, and he glitched like a spyware ridden HoloPop. I grabbed his twitching body and hoisted him for a shield against the grey HCPD uniforms beating toward me with their plasma rifles drawn.

"On the ground, Marlowe," shouted the front man. "You can't afford to lose any more body parts."

I used my upgrade to keep my core covered with the bro's limp braincase and backed into the queue slowly. The piece was mint and Rae's installation rated, but my nerves screamed beneath the prosthetic as I strained past its lifting threshold. The lead officer stopped running and locked his sights in my direction. I pushed through a group of upper-crust wastrels and let them fill in the gap between me and the uniforms. Shooting into a crowd of bystanders on the Grit strip wouldn't phase HCPD, but the *Island Dreamer* subset would be uglied up with lawyers before the smell of ozone cleared. Swain wouldn't put up with that for a grid-streak minute.

Fuming socialites and Biz District suits glared at me with

money dripping from every pore and crystalizing in their eyes. There was no way I was getting on the bangtail now, but I still had enough cush to scatter the old-fashioned way. The trick would be to lose the goons long enough to hightail it to a fast bird or sneak on the next slug. Stairs hit the back of my heels when I made it to the outer perimeter of the bangtail station. I stumbled under the weight of the techhead and his mountain of gear. The crowd had closed around me, protecting me temporarily from the greys, so I let his body fall and hoped he wouldn't have too many bootprints on his pretty face when he woke up. I turned to force my way through the sea of dirty cush in designer handbags, hoping I could cut past the doors and back toward the slug without any uniforms catching on to my drift, when something hit the back of my neck like a guillotine.

My knees buckled and my upgrade twitched. I rolled my eyes around the crowd, trying to figure out which one of the weasels had hit me. Someone hefted me to my feet and let me hang there in a titanium grip. "Over here, officers, I got her!"

Bug-Eye's pal, back from his vacation in Glitch City, I guessed. I kicked backward at him but only managed to hurt my foot. How could he move under all that gear? He crushed my arms against my torso, pinning my upgrade uselessly into my side, and stars burst in on my view like uninvited party guests. The crowd parted for a unit of HoloCity's finest to shove their way v-form through the outraged queue.

"Let go, citizen." The front man, a vice official I vaguely

recognized, pinned me with his rifle. "And step back. We've got her now."

My captor loosened his grip and I flexed my upgrade, but he snatched me back before I could give him a kiss. "Is there a reward for handing her over?"

"Drop her." The grey used his big boy voice and let his sights wander a little higher, as if to say his aim might not be all that great. "And step back."

"Not even a thank you?" The techhead had found his metal cojones and proceeded to stuff them down his own throat. "'Cause I don't like having to do your job for you, bro."

I ducked my head and a subordinate officer nailed buddy with a blast from the stun gun. His titanium grip melted. I hit the deck and rolled into the wave of screaming socialites trying to high-pitch their way out of the line of fire.

The grey cursed, and I heard the firing officer licking boots while the rest of them tried to break up the panic with more stunners. Bodies dressed in designer rags draped over red-velvet queue markers and rolled to the damp cobblestones. The greys hollered over the squealers, threatening them back into a sense of tranquillity. "Resisting compliance with HCPD officers is classified as Tier 3 Civil Disobedience, punishable by fines of up to 5K and the possibility of jail time. Please remain calm."

A shot rang out over the commons like a backfiring bangtail, and the rioting skipped a beat. All eyes were on a huge, black man in a sleek, white admiral's uniform. He swept aside the rabble with one ham-sized fist and a small cannon smoking in the other. "What is the meaning of this?"

The leader of the greys leered at the admiral with ill-disguised contempt. "You have a fugitive trying to board your space craft. Sir."

The admiral scanned the crowd and homed in on me where I was crab-walking through the forest of class sticks in stilettos and shiny-toed grid slickers. His voice boomed out of a chest like a bass drum, "Betty 'Bubbles' Marlowe?"

Busted. Called by the name my mama gave me and everything. I pushed myself back onto my feet and tried to regain a fraction of my dignity, if I'd ever had any. "Yes, sir."

"Come with me, please." The big man turned and pointed himself toward the entrance of the bangtail station. I hesitated just long enough to count the eggs in my basket before I tossed them all out and followed the white shoulders of the behemoth fleet master.

"Wait just a minute, Admiral!" The grey's voice climbed up a notch and trembled at the edge. "We have a warrant for her—"

The admiral spun again and pointed the cannon over my shoulder at the V of grey uniforms behind me. His hand didn't waver. "HCPD has no jurisdiction here. Unless you want me to make a very unpleasant call to Chief Swain about his losses in the line of duty, I suggest you take your officers off my sward and apologize to my guests on your way out."

The grey burned a hole in the back of my head with a laser glare. I basked in its warmth with a smile on my lips as I let myself be swept into the admiral's wake. The greys backed off and ruffled cush feathers settled into place as everyone made their way back into neat little lines, sobered by the appearance of the man in white. Minor *Dream* fleet officers rushed to open the doors into the glass station building for the admiral, and I slipped quietly inside after him. The officers flanked him in perfect synchronization, tattlers flashing navigation charts and lists of passengers and supplies. He listened silently and coasted his way through the building.

I had never been inside a bangtail station before, but I'd done all the HoloPop tours while in the dregs of a hangover, choking on the bitterness of lost dreams. Every surface gleamed with chrome and white in testament to the stacks of cush an operation like that burned through, as evidenced by the custodial costs alone. At the centre of the main floor, customer-service representatives in crisp, sky-blue uniforms and neat white caps sorted passengers between the shuttle fleet with the speed and precision of dealers in a high-stakes card game. Curved metal staircases glittered and twisted their way toward a pyramid of mirrored glass on the floor above. The admiral climbed the stairs on the left, and his entourage dropped like flies without him saying a word. I didn't know what else to do, so I kept following.

"Step into my office, Marlowe," the admiral said at the top of the stairs. His voice reverberated off the mirrored glass and left a hum in the air. He opened the door and strode inside.

I stepped in after him and followed him to the massive, white desk at the centre of the room. How a man like that knew my name I could only guess, but the way he snatched me out of Swain's sweaty grasp could only be a blessing. Or so I thought.

"What can I do for you, sir?"

He leaned into a high-backed chair that looked like it might have been made from genuine elephant hide. I don't know what else would have been big enough. Then he fixed me with a look harder than diamonds and said, "You and I have a serious problem."

CHAPTER 7

"A problem, sir?" I dry-swallowed the rock in my esophagus. "If you mean that nonsense about the warrant I—"

"Do you know who I am, Marlowe?" The admiral leaned back in the rough grey leather chair and spun sideways so that it looked like he wasn't watching me. In the reflection from the mirror glass wall on the far side of the room, his black eyes stared unblinkingly at the side of my face. He had a smattering of grey in his neatly trimmed beard and at his temples and looked to be a man at the top of his prime. Shoulders like boulders heaved beneath the sharp-white uniform, and a neck as thick as one of my thighs flexed as he swallowed.

I pretended not to notice him watching me in the glass. "I

know you're an admiral, sir."

"Admiral Hollard of the *Dream* fleet franchise," he said without pride, just a matter-of-fact. "Including the *Sweet Dream*, *Fever Dream*, *Dream On*, and the *Island Dreamer* on which you seem to have been awarded passage for the inaugural voyage. Quite a prestigious honour for an ex-Grit District beat cop with a phony P.I. ticket and a questionable source for cybernetic equipment."

I flexed the long pink fingers of my upgrade and showed him the paperwork. "It's a prototype. Special contract."

"Spare me, Marlowe." Hollard eased his chair around to face me and leaned forward on his desk with fingers as thick and black as street cart blood sausages. "I'm not interested in your tickets or how you managed to land yourself on one of my ships. What I want to know about is your connection to this woman."

Admiral Hollard killed the lights and brought up a 'gram of my client's "sister" with her head and necklace still attached. I clenched my fist and tried to figure my chances if I jumped through the mirror glass and back out the station door. Dead within seconds, probably. "I was hired to find her, but someone punched her card before I got there. Now Swain's trying to knock me up on murder charges."

"Chief Swain is a lot of hot air wrapped in a poorly fitted suit." Admiral Hollard slammed a palm against his desk and leaned back in his chair again. I swallowed an inappropriate noise. "And those charges won't even hold the sludge they call seawater around here. This woman is on one of my ships right now. The *Island Dreamer,* as a matter-of-fact."

"That can't be, sir." I stared at the hologram as it faded out and was replaced by a live feed. My girl, necklace and all, throwing her head back in a laugh and tossing dice across a green-felt table. "I saw her body."

The admiral's face hardened into the sculpted mask of a Trade War Era statue. "You saw wrong."

"Yes, sir," I said. What else could I say? If one of us was going to be wrong, it had better be me. "So what do you need me for?"

"I have been made a generous offer by a … person of import … who knows the woman is alive and well aboard the *Island Dreamer* and who would like to see her stay that way." The admiral stood and crossed his arms behind his back. He strode out from behind the desk and loomed above me. I kept my eyes on the blank wall ahead of me and told my heart to stop beating so loudly. "I have more than enough security to manage that."

"Of course, sir."

"I want to know who this woman is, and why she's worth so much." The admiral leaned toward me like a toppling siege tower. I fought the urge to leap out of his way. "You're going to find out for me."

"And Chief Swain's warrant—"

"Will make a trip down his throat if he tries that half-rate number with me again." Admiral Hollard clapped his big hands and broke the sound barrier. "Consider it your payment for services rendered."

A gentle knock at the door allowed me to turn my head. I took a deep breath and stepped out of the admiral's shadow, feeling a bit lighter and bit braver. With Chief Swain neutralized and a new job on the roster, it looked like I might just survive to see next week after all.

A tall, thin man stepped into the room wearing an equally crisp but deep-blue uniform with silver buttons up the front of it. A red-skinned face, creased and weathered by too many years of poorly filtered UV rays, perched atop his narrow shoulders like a shrunken head in a curios shop.

"Who's the pepperoni stick?" I muttered out of the side of my mouth, earning me a hard lined mouth from the admiral.

"This is Hank Whyte, Chief of Security on the *Island Dreamer*." The Admiral placed a hand on my left shoulder and squeezed so hard enugh I thought he'd dent the upgrade. "You'll be reporting to him for the duration of our cruise. Enjoy your holiday."

He pushed me toward my new keeper and returned to his desk. Whyte nodded his well-smoked face at me, and his skin folded back around his too-bright teeth. He held the door open like a gentleman corpse.

"Nice to meet you, Hank," I said as he ushered me out the door.

"And Marlowe"—the Admiral's voice boomed out of the room after me—"Don't give me cause to regret our alliance. As an enemy, I would make Swain look like a sweet potato."

CHAPTER 8

"**G**reat," I said as Hank Whyte, Chief of Security, led me back down the glittering staircase toward the check-in desk. "Now I'm hungry."

"You don't want to bite Admiral Sweet Potato." Whyte kept his eyes straight ahead and his mouth a hard line. "Trust me."

But the corner of his weathered lip twitched, and I laughed. "I might like you after all."

"There will be refreshments available on the shuttle," Whyte said as he guided me in front of one of the sky-blue uniformed attendants in the crisp white caps. She had pale-blonde hair pinned in a neat bun at the nape of her neck, a sun-kissed complexion, and big Chiclet teeth to match her hat. She asked for my name through her cushy dental work and looked right through me. A suit in the queue we'd cut cleared his throat loudly. Whyte ignored him.

"That's more like it." I gave the attendant my name, and she keyed it into the system with pink, almond-shaped fingernails that swept through the air with practiced graceful arcs. "I was looking forward to a vacation, you know."

"We can discuss the details of your contract on the shuttle," Whyte said, nodding to the woman. "You'll be flying with me."

"Door three, please, ma'am." Her voice was only slightly tight when she said it. What a professional. "And please enjoy your time as an *Island Dreamer*."

I turned to say something to Whyte, but he had evaporated into the crowd, so I stepped around the counter. Behind the service desk, six, round doorways were lit with white neon tubes that emanated a soft, bluish light, each with a tastefully arranged collection of dots above it to indicate which door was which. I stepped through the third gate and into a glowing white corridor with floor lights leading the way toward the shuttles. A mirrored door shushed open at the end of the corridor, and I stepped through to a security checkpoint.

Once the doors closed behind me, and I was hidden from the other passengers, two grim-faced officials peeled themselves off the wall and approached me with scan wands drawn. It was nice that they gave their customers some privacy for the necessary prodding. Nicer still if security had to get tough. Wouldn't want to spoil the start of anyone's vacation with blood spray and missing teeth. I knew the play. Despite the official invite from the admiral, anxiety clawed at my chest, and I had to fight to control my breathing.

"Please remove any and all cybernetic enhancements, external techwear, or other inorganic devices from your person and place them on the conveyor belt to your left." The official droned robotically, probably for the thousandth time that day. "Or, if you so choose, you may take the tunnel."

I dropped my backpack, jacket, and umbrella on the belt. "The tunnel?"

"If your technology is difficult to remove or implanted internally, you may enter the immersive scanning tunnel."

"Let's do that."

"This way, ma'am," the other security guard said in an equally robotic voice. "I must advise you that if you are carrying or wearing any illegal technology such as explosives, firearms, or toxins of any kind they will be removed and destroyed and you will be held for questioning. We do not accept any legal responsibility for the cost of replacing destroyed technologies, and in the case of implanted devices, we cannot guarantee your physical safety in the tunnel."

I swallowed. Rae hadn't shown me everything the arm was capable of before I rushed out of the office. I had no idea what kind of tech might be embedded in the prosthesis. "Can't I just show you my ticket?"

The security officer's bland smile made the hairs on the back of my neck stand on end and icy fingers trail across my shoulders. "That won't be necessary."

Of course not. Watching illegal implants get ripped out of cush-drunk passengers' bodies was probably the highlight of his day.

A narrow door parallel to the main corridor opened silently beside the officer. Inside, it was pitch black and smooth as eel skin. A bead of cold sweat trickled from my forehead and past my ear. The white jumpsuit clung to my skin and itched in undignified places. I rolled my shoulders once. The nerve connection was seamless. Rae had outdone herself this time. There was no way I would be able to get the arm connected properly on my own, even if the security creeps deigned to help me.

I took in a deep breath of air, stretching my lungs until they burned, and then let it out slowly through my nostrils. I stepped inside.

"Please proceed to the end of the tunnel," the man said with a glint of suppressed joy in his colourless eyes. "In the event of your inability to do so under your own power, assistance will be provided. Do we have your consent to intervene?"

My mouth said "yes," but the word disappeared before I heard it. Either the audio equipment inside the tunnel was more sensitive than my ears, or security didn't actually give a steaming Grit pile about my consent, because the door closed behind me, leaving me in total darkness. A fraction of a second later, lights flashed on with a simulated banging noise that must have been there just to make the tunnel walkers feel extra guilty. The long, narrow throat pulsed with red and purple light, and the scanning equipment thrummed behind the walls.

"Please proceed," a voice boomed through an overhead speaker system. I thought I detected a malicious smile behind the voice, but that could have been my imagination. Just in case, I flexed my fingers and imagined giving the smarmy officer a kiss with my fist. Then I stepped into the light.

The humming noise intensified as I got farther into the tunnel, one slow step at a time. My upgrade vibrated unnervingly and felt hot against my slick skin. I kept moving forward. All I had to do was make it to the end of the tunnel, right? Sweat rolled between my shoulder blades and pooled in the curve of my back. I took another step forward. And another.

The pain started in the severed nerve endings at the end of my stump. Electric shocks of bright, hot pain shot up the side of my neck and directly into my brain. The metal glowed as red as a hot poker under the throbbing lights of the tunnel, and the flesh around my shoulder felt like it was being seared by an iron. Almost there. I kept moving forward.

When I reached the end of the tunnel, my entire body felt raw and blistered. Even my eyeballs burned. The door opened, and I stepped into the cool white light with a groan. The air outside the tunnel splashed across my scalded skin like an ice bath.

"Congratulations." The security official did a swell job of keeping the disappointment from his voice. "You have been cleared for shuttle access to board the *Island Dreamer*."

"Is it supposed to hurt like that?" I inspected my real arm and was surprised to see healthy, pale-pink flesh instead of the blisters and boils of a radiation burn.

The officer gave me a blank look. "It's new."

I flexed my upgrade to make sure none of the joints had melted or seized. "It was like a trial by fire."

"We do not encourage the use of cybernetic technologies aboard the fleet of *Dreams*." He intoned officially. "Perhaps next time you will choose to forgo your enhancements for the duration of your stay with us."

I marked a spot on his chin and balled up my fist. Then I laughed. "Tell that to the techheads in line behind me."

"We look forward to the opportunity." The second security officer handed me my jacket and backpack and stood with my umbrella tucked under his arm. "Please enjoy your time as an *Island Dreamer*."

"What a way to start a vacation." I snatched my gear and pushed between the two security guards toward the circular gate at the end of the white corridor. The door shushed open quietly and Whyte's sunburned face greeted me.

"I figured out why you look like a stick of smoked meat," I said. "Do you have to walk through the crucible of flame every time you board a shuttle?"

"That should not have been necessary." He narrowed his

icy-blue eyes, the weathered flesh around them hardened into a starburst of deeply carved lines. "The admiral granted you a security pass."

"The sadistic duo in there failed to get the memo." I pulled my jacket over my shoulders and kicked the door to the security check. My boot bounced off without leaving a mark. I cracked my knuckles against my metallic palm. "Want me to go back in and deliver it for you?"

"I will see to it," Whyte said perfunctorily, his eyes peering at his reflection in the glass as if he could see through the mirrored surface.

"I don't mind. Really." A chill had settled over my skin after the heat of the tunnel. I shook out my arms and bounced on my toes. "I could use the warm up if we're going to be sitting for… How long is the shuttle trip?"

"A few hours," Whyte said. "Depending on where in its orbit the *Island Dreamer* is. But you will be able to move freely except during the take off and docking procedures."

"And there will be food?"

"It is a catered flight." Whyte led the way farther down the corridor through another set of mirrored doors. "You will be quite comfortable."

"I'm flying with you?" I swung the umbrella around my hand once and then ditched it next to the doors. Not much rain on a space cruise, I figured. "How many cush rollers per bangtail?"

"We do not refer to our customers as 'cush rollers.'"

"There's got to be a lot of holocred pinging on a cruise like this," I said. "I'm surprised the delicate upper crust allows themselves to be subjected to the tunnel treatment back there."

"That scanner is a new feature," Whyte said. "And it is meant to be used only in extreme cases. I'm afraid our officers may have been too eager to try out their new toy. Normally, on other voyages, such stringent procedures are not necessary at all. But we have a special guest aboard the *Island Dreamer* for this inaugural flight."

The pieces clicked into place and my eyes widened. "Fade out, Whyte. You're ribbing me up."

He gave me a sideways look. "I don't know what that means."

"The dusty-pink robes, the anti-tech screening, the 'person of import'…" I counted out my points on ragged nailed fingers. "You're hosting the head weirdo of the Last Humanists on the *Dreamer*?"

"First of all, the head weirdo's title is 'The Rose.'" Whyte said. "Second, that would be most unlikely. Wouldn't it?"

"Is he the one who's interested in the silver lady?"

"I'm sure I have no idea." Whyte keyed his code into a door so covered with touchscreens and buttons it was impossible to tell where it was going to open from. "Your job is to find out who she is, not who wants to keep her alive."

I rolled my eyes behind his back. "The two could be related, you know."

A crack opened horizontally through the centre of the door and the parts slid into the ceiling and floor, respectively. We stepped into a massive, open-hanger space, the air heavy with the high-octane brain buzz of rocket fuel and hot metal. Six shuttles the size of Biz District office towers cocked and loaded and ready for liftoff. Six doors like the one we just passed through opened and closed at intervals as customers made their way through security and into the hanger. Transparent fencing guided the guests toward their designated spacecraft in efficiently straight lines. Most of the clientele plugged their noses and picked up the pace as if trying to forget the grease and gears that powered the façade of the luxurious star-cruising lifestyles of the rich and famous.

I put a crick in my neck trying to see everything at once. "I've been known to get a glow-on in the past, but I never drifted into anything like this."

Chief of Security Hank Whyte smiled his cracked leather smile. He guided me toward a bangtail shuttle worth more cush than I could wrap my rocket-fuel fuzzed brain around. He said, "There is nothing else like this."

"It's a marvel of human ingenuity," I said. "Space travel. I mean, I knew it. But I didn't know it like this."

"You have to see it to believe it." Whyte stood aside to let me climb the white metal stairs up to the wide-open doors of the bangtail. The words *Whippet 3* were in sharp relief against the cold, silver gleam of the shuttle in stark black paint.

"I must be the luckiest Grit in HoloCity"—I tripped on the first step and smashed my elbow on the handrail—"or this whole dizzy dream is going to come crashing down on my head."

"I'm beginning to like you, Ms. Marlowe." Whyte helped me back up to my feet with his ruddy face close to mine. "But the dream is already crashing, and unless you can help us, not even the admiral will be able to stop the pot from boiling over."

CHAPTER 9

The blur of the last few hours took a toll on me and after I had been fed and watered—real, filtered, lunar water, blissfully tasteless, in clear blue recyclable bottles that each cost more than I made in a month—I stretched out in my fully adjustable seat, grabbed a complimentary blanket, and waited for sleep to take me away on the best trip money can't buy.

Whyte's cryptic remark as we boarded the bangtail barely registered in my awe at seeing the interior of the shuttle. Pearlescent white and pastels seemed to be the fashion of the day. Blocks of seats were arranged like private sitting rooms. White chairs and loungers in melting geometric shapes clustered around glass tables. As the last passengers boarded the shuttle, people settled into the groups they were travelling with. Smaller pods joined with others that looked like suitable companions for the journey, the way the extroverted tended to do when away from their usual sets, and the introverted were dragged along with them.

Whyte had deposited me in an empty block before he'd faded away to attend to some professional duty or other. He'd explained it to me, but the words flew straight by on the fast bird while my over-stimulated Grit-scrub brain sat there like a lump of primordial ooze. I think I nodded to him before I let the dream world of the space shuttle fly me to the stars.

In my white jumpsuit I laid back, flipped down my glasses, and did my best to look like another piece of furniture. For a while, I listened to the buzz of conversation around me and admired the way the cush set talked about absolutely nothing in such excruciating detail. It didn't take me long to decide there was nothing to be gained by keeping my eyes peeled, so I closed them and let the buzz slip away beneath the white noise in my shades.

I didn't know what woke me, but I killed the sound in the tubes and opened my ears. My neck ached from where the girl in silver had stung me with the sleeper drug. I rubbed at it absently. Still swollen. I kept the glasses on. A drunken couple had stumbled into the block of seats I had had to myself. They fumbled at one another awkwardly, forgetting the privacy screen or too far gone to care about discretion. I kept my glasses on, killed the white noise, and listened. A sharp, hissing whisper cut through the grunts and moans of the groping pair. I focused my attention that way.

"—can't be. How could he, with the warrant plastered all over the feeds?" said a woman's voice, coming from the block behind my seat.

"Don't ask me," a lilting male voice replied in hushed urgency. "I don't invent the gossip, I just spread it."

"There's a reward, you know," she said. "For information. You could make a quick stack with a tip like that."

"I have enough cush to choke a highbinder politician," he said primly. "I'm not interested in any rewards. What I want is a crack at that punch, the real stuff. Not the cut batch that's circulating right now."

The woman forgot their secrecy and laughed like a trained seal. "So what, you're going to suss him out and throw a pile of holocred in his lap?"

"Shut your sausage hole, Lindy!" A dainty slapping sound and more giggling. "You want to blow it for me before I even have a chance? I'd share the glow with you."

"You're serious?" The whisper was back. "You'd slide up to Punch Blanco and make an offer like that?"

"Why not? Now that he's been made by the HCPD, he's got to be hard for cush. Maybe he needs a friend with a fat roll?"

"You'd love that, wouldn't you," she teased, but her voice had tightened around the edges.

"I won't have to talk to him if my sources are on the level," he said. "It's the drops. Perfectly safe."

"Safe, my Holy Origin. They'll find your fish-nibbled corpse in the harbour, you dizzy vetch."

"I take it back, I'm not sharing with you." Petulant now. "Forget I said anything."

"Don't do it, Ted," she implored. "We can have a good time with what we brought along. Security let me keep the uppers and we have—"

"Forget it, I said." He stood up noisily. "Let's go get a drink."

They moved away from the block as I peered between the seats, but they disappeared into a cloud of milling socialites before I got a good look. I flipped up my visilenses and folded my blanket. The grunting couple had fallen into a stupor on the floor, hands still half-heartedly grabbing bits of flesh but no longer knowing what to do with it. I shook the blanket out again and spread it over them, hoping to ease the flood of anxiety they'd wake with as their bodies flushed out whatever poisons they'd ingested. It was hard to feel too sorry for wastrels with more cred than sense, but I hoped for their sakes that they would at least remember where they were and knew the person they were with when they woke. No amount of cush can ease the existential dread of sobriety after a hard roll in the glow.

"How have you found the trip so far?" Hank Whyte's low baritone rumbled behind me. I turned, and his neat, blue suit was like an anchor in the surrounding sea of pastel, white, and chrome.

"I slept."

"I know," he said. "I've been waiting for you to wake up. I wanted to show you the viewing deck before we dock up to *Island Dreamer*. Would you like something to drink?"

I held up my water bottle. "Don't they have viewing decks on the cruiser?"

"Not like on the shuttle." Whyte polished a silver button on his wrist with the cuff on his other arm, his eyes sliding across the room with the casual attentiveness of a professional observer. "Some of the cushier suites have private viewing areas, but most passengers don't cruise for the views. They get their fill of that on the bangtail and then spend the rest of their trip hopping from holobeach to dance club."

"They could do that in HoloCity."

Whyte's sunburned face cracked ruefully. "Yes, but it wouldn't cost as much."

"Show me." I stretched out the tight spots and then grabbed my things. "I might spend most of my time on a holobeach too."

"You're more likely to find the admiral's woman in question in the clubs and gambling rooms." Whyte strode out of the common area and down a hallway at the outer edge of the shuttle.

"He doesn't expect me to work 24/7, does he?" I run my fingers along the smooth white wall of the corridor. "I'm supposed to be on vacation."

"The admiral is the kind of man who works day and night with little rest." Whyte said. "He knows better than to hold others to his own standard. Still, I suggest you don't disappoint him."

"Sweet Potato Swain. I remember."

Round doors, each with an expansive key code system out front, lined the hallway to our right. To my left, with only a few feet of metal and wires and whatever else makes up a spacecraft's shell between us and it, was the great empty space that had fascinated human beings for as long as our primitive brains could fathom worlds beyond our own. Even without being able to see it, a feeling like vertigo hit me. With artificial gravity and no earth or sky to tell the difference, we could have been flying upside down and I wouldn't know. There was no upside down unless some goon held you by the ankles before he beat you.

At the end of the corridor, we came to a glass door like the ones at the bangtail station. Whyte did his little dance with the security system, and the circular door made a hissing noise as it broke into triangular pieces and twisted away from the centre, widening like the pupil of a pinch on the glow. Inside was outer space.

The walls, some synthetic material as clear as glass, wrapped us in a bubble of breathable air that seemed to protrude from the side of the shuttle with nothing above or below us. A handful of observers floated through the stars ahead of us with small sweep-and-buff bots zipped across the surface behind them, ensuring that no smudge or smears would interfere with the guest's viewing experience.

"The deck is closing for maintenance." Whyte's deep voice

resonated strangely in the open space. "Please avail yourselves of the refreshments in the commons. We will dock within the hour."

The passengers filed out obediently, with Whyte and I standing on either side of the round door like sentinels. Once they were gone, he stepped out onto the deck and held out an elbow for me, like an old-fashioned gentleman. I didn't normally go for that kind of thing, but it was surprisingly reassuring in that void-like space. My heart hammered in my ears as my boot hovered above the transparent floor and the stars gleamed below.

"It's perfectly safe," Whyte assured me. Just like getting punched by Blanco's best.

I closed my eyes and let my foot drop. Vertigo surged in my chest and then my boot connected with the floor and I stepped out toward Whyte. The door shushed closed behind me and the mechanical locks engaged with a click. I took his elbow and tried not to bruise his arm. Once I was firmly attached and more or less convinced I wouldn't float off into the ether, we moved toward the outer edge of the viewing bubble.

Below us a streak of orange and gold marked an edge of Tigris, the spiral galaxy that our Terra Firma called home. "There's so much colour," I said when I finally had words to speak. "From the surface it all looks black and white. Nothing is ever that simple, I guess."

"Galaxies, like the hoary breath of long-dead gods," Whyte said as if he were quoting something.

Movement caught my eye in the blackness above Tigris'

stripe. Blinking white and red lights, dull and lifeless compared to the natural competition of their surroundings, trailed through the stars just ahead of us. "What is that?"

"The *Island Dreamer.*"

"It's running away from us."

"The shuttles use most of their power to get themselves close to the same orbit as the cruiser," Whyte explained. "Then we use the last of the fuel to catch the dock."

"What if you miss?"

He laughed, but grimly. "We never miss."

"If you say so." I got brave and touched the surface of the viewing lens with the tips of my fingers. "This rates, Whyte. But I'm still looking forward to the holobeaches. I've never been to one, real or virtual."

"You don't get many vacations in your line of work?"

"I don't get much money in my line of work," I said. "This kind of thing is way outside my pay grade. I'm only here because I won the Lucky Bastard Sweepstakes."

"I see." Whyte took a thin, black cigar out of his pocket and lit it with a sulphur match. Yellow-grey haze spiralled up from the end of it and dissipated as if into the stars. "How fortunate, for the *Dream* fleet as well as for you."

"What's the smoke, Whyte?" I asked. "Why'd you really bring me here?"

Whyte's calm professionalism hardened into something else, something cold and brittle. "The universe is both simple and complex, and never exactly what it seems."

I flexed my upgrade against my thigh and watched him from my peripheral vision. "If there's something you want to say to me, then say it. Earlier you wanted to talk about something. The dream was crashing down, you said. What did you mean, and what does any of this have to do with me?"

"You tell me." Whyte blew twin streams of smoke out of his cracked terracotta nostrils and curled his lip. "Because something about this stinks, and you're the monkey in the middle of it all."

"Your guess is as good as mine." The acrid smog burned the back of my throat. I took out a piece of gum, peeled it, and popped it into my mouth. "If you want to hear my version, I'll give it to you. See if you can make sense of it."

"Don't leave out the funny bits."

"The only thing funny about my life is the fact that I'm not dead yet." I blew a big pink bubble and sucked it in through my teeth with a snap. "And Swain is trying his best to square up that account."

"I like you, Marlowe." Whyte flicked a worm of ash onto the floor and one of the scrubber bots zipped over to buzz around his feet. "I don't like many people, but you seem like you're on the level. Still, there're some things that don't add up and depending on how you answer me right now, you might spend your vacation in my lock up."

"And here I thought we were friends, Hank."

Whyte grinned with a set of bleached white teeth that gleamed like raw bone in his withered face. "What do you know about the woman the admiral is interested in?"

"I know the last time I saw her there was a little too much space between her shoulders and her head."

"And yet she is on my ship." He snorted and spat, and the bots scrubbed that up too. I was beginning to see why he liked the viewing deck. He said, "Why were you looking for her?"

"A couple weeks ago, I get a call from a lady using a voice scrambler—could be she's not a lady at all, but let's pretend—and she wants me to find her sister, wants me to deliver a message. I get an anonymous 'gram on my tattler, a girl. Not much of a silver cocktail dress, a pretty little choker. So I tracked her down as a dancer at techRose, a real silk joint tucked into the gritty centre of the city. You should try it some time."

"So, what's a pro skirt from the Grit District doing tossing dice on the *Island Dreamer*?" Whyte grimaced. "Our clientele are out of her league."

"That's your concern? The clientele isn't as different as you'd like to think, once they've got a good glow going. What about the fact that the last time I saw her someone had taken pains to remove her head from her body?"

"It doesn't add up," he said again. Then he dropped the stub of his cigar on the deck and ground it out with his heel before the bots got to it.

"I don't know what you want me to tell you."

"You just happen to win a stay in our most expensive suite thanks to the generous vice doctors at Lucky Bastard, and the admiral just happens to receive word from his contact that this woman is on one of his ships and is to be kept alive at all costs, and I just happen to find one of your business cards in—"

"The universe works in mysterious ways." I snapped my gum. "And I don't have business cards."

"What did you do to piss off Swain?"

"You looking to tell him I'm singing songs?"

"He's no friend of mine," Whyte said. "I just like to know what I'm up against."

"I asked the wrong kind of questions about the wrong kind of case," I said. "I got to see what my insides look like, misplaced an arm, and earned an early retirement over it. I made a promise not to get involved in the wrong kind of cases anymore, and I've kept that promise. Seems its not good enough for Señor Sweet Potato."

"What does the silver lady have to do with the case Swain wants hushed up?"

"If I thought there was a connection, I wouldn't have taken the case." I slammed my palm against the glass and felt the sting travel reassuringly up my arm. "I'd like to keep this one."

"Alright, here's another question for you." Whyte took out

another cigar and stuck it between his lips. It hung there, unlit, wagging like the tail of an excited puppy while he talked. "You ever play the Lucky Bastard Sweepstakes? Or are the vice doctors handing out tickets to every skid mark in HoloCity just to make my life miserable?"

"Not so long ago, you said you liked me." I made a point of my finger with my metal arm, placed it on the top of my head, and did a little twirl like a mechanical dancer. "What's the matter? You don't like the show?"

"Your story stinks."

"It was the best I could do on short notice," I said. "You want a neat little lie that checks all the boxes and leaves no unanswered questions, you've got to give a girl some time."

He sighed and rubbed his eyes with the back of one hand. "I don't want any lies."

"How about a tip, instead?" I passed him a piece of gum. "Quit the sticks. They'll stunt your growth and ruin your complexion."

He took the cigar out of his mouth and held it in the palm of his hand next to the gum, staring at them as if he was having a crisis of faith. "I shouldn't have said that. About the dream crashing down."

"Look, Hank. I know it doesn't make any sense. I've been wracking my brains over it for the last twenty-four hours. But the fact is, the truth usually doesn't make sense until you've got some distance from it. I'm on the level, and I'd like to help you if I can. So tell me, what did you mean?"

"Maybe nothing," he said. "Maybe I meant it's my dream. I thought there was a connection, but…"

"Well, don't hold out on me now." I wrapped my arm around his shoulder and whispered in his hear. "I'm told I'm very easy to talk to."

He pushed my arm away and wiped some imaginary dust off his epaulettes. "We had an incident reported earlier in the day. It's no longer an issue."

"You sure?" I said. "You seemed pretty worried before."

"I needn't have been," he said. "At least, not about that."

"You play pretty coy for an ugly man."

Whyte's lips made a thin line in his weathered red face. He tapped his jacket pocket on the left side, over his heart. "I found your business card hidden in my wife's underwear drawer."

"Even if I had business cards"—I crossed my arms over my chest and glared at him—"I'd be giving you the look right now."

"Give this 'the look.'" He took out a thin, pink card from his pocket and flicked it at me.

The metal fingers of my cybernetic hand pinched the card out of the air before I knew I was thinking about it. The upgrade lived up to its name. I laid the card flat on my palm and a 'gram of my face popped up and hovered in the air between us with the words BUBBLES MARLOWE: PRIVATE INVESTIGATOR blinking below it. I growled. "Dickie."

"I want to know what she contacted you about," Whyte said. "If it has anything to do with the silver woman, I need to know."

I spat my gum into the wrapper and tossed it for the scrubber bots to chase after. "Who is your wife?"

"Patricia Whyte," Whyte said. "Patti. She was a scientist with Libra."

"I have friends with Libra." Then I remembered Jimi. "One, anyway. In MedEx."

"I wondered how you could afford a grip like that."

"It's a prototype," I said. "I signed a waiver and promised not to sue if it short-circuits my brain."

"Relax," he said. "I don't need to see your papers."

"Why do you say she 'was' a scientist?" I asked. "Libra is the silk for petri dish pushers. Why'd she leave?"

"I'd love to know that, too, if you're going to give me the goods. About a year ago, she quit suddenly and insisted on travelling with me on the cruisers," Whyte said. "At first I was thrilled to spend more time with her. We'd only been married a few months, but—"

"She's not the same person you married."

He nodded grimly. "If she ever was."

"And you want me to tell you what she's up to?"

"I knew something like this might happen."

"You're the Chief of Security on the biggest luxury cruiser in our trade zone," I said. "And you don't trust your own wife?"

"She's high class, beautiful, smart. What does she see in a guy like me?"

"A million dollar personality?"

"Few cred short on that charge, I'm afraid. I'm a fool," he said. "But I love her."

"You must have believed she loved you, once, too."

"Maybe I wanted to believe it for a little while."

"And now?"

"Now I want to know what she hired you for and who she's meeting at 1900 hours tomorrow night."

"You're not going to whack her if you don't like the answer, are you?"

"No," he said. "I'm not the jealous type. I know the cards I was dealt, and I'll play them as best I can. I just want a glimpse at her hand, know what I'm up against."

"You've said that before." I took out another stick of gum. "You a gambling man, Chief?"

"I've been known to take a few long shots."

"Well, I hate to disappoint you, but I don't like your odds on this one."

"You're not the one who has to pay the bookie, Marlowe," he said. "So tell me. What do you know?"

"Your wife never contacted me, Hank." I tucked the business card into my pocket and made a mental note to tear Dickie a new bung hole the next time I talked to him. Tough to stay under the radar when your face is in the pants of every punter whose wife fell asleep under a table and couldn't find her way home. "I can't guess what she's up to any better than you can, but if it would help you sleep at night I can keep an eye on her for you."

"I can live with her having secrets," he said. "I just want to know she's safe."

"You ever hear of Punch Blanco?"

Whyte's face stiffened into a mask of petrified wood. "The mobster? Sure. Why do you ask?"

I shrugged and snapped my gum in the silence hanging awkwardly between us. "What's his connection?"

"Is there one?"

"Look, you want me to play it straight with you I need you to do me the same courtesy. I heard a couple of glow chasers out in the lounge gossiping about Blanco being on board the *Island Dreamer*. Figured he was here to push some juice. Swain's got his pecker in a twist over this new drug, and I've already lost all the skin I had in it. If you're asking me to—"

"I don't know anything about him." Whyte finally tucked the cigar into his pocket and unwrapped the gum. "But I know his mug. He's in our system. So, unless he's got some state-of-the-art skin our scan cams can't see through, he's not on the *Island*

Dreamer."

"So why'd you look like you felt something slimy in your pants when I said his name?"

Whyte's jaw flexed as he mawed on the pink stick, and his eyes slid sideways to me. "You've got the manners of a Grit skid alright."

I just waited. Sometimes that's all it takes.

"Punch Blanco isn't the kind of mug I'd notice," he said. "I don't watch the news reels. The ship gets the 'Most Wanted' lists from HoloCity, but I just feed them into the computer and let them do their jobs. I wouldn't have noticed him except for the look Patti gets on her face every time he pops up on the feeds. Like someone walking over her grave."

"You think she could be using Tropical Punch?"

He shook his head sharply as if to shake the words right back out his ear. "No. She's not on the glow."

"You sure? That's the kind of info that might be worth my life if it gets back to Sweetie Swain."

Whyte chewed his gum thoughtfully. He said, "He can't touch you here."

The back of my neck itched when he said that. I looked over my shoulder, suddenly paranoid that he might have someone watching me right now. Then I shook my head. Swain's racket down in HoloCity was tight, no question about that. But he didn't rate high enough on the command chain to send goons into outer space just to harass me.

"No jurisdiction," I said. "Sure. But he's not going to forget about me now that the admiral stepped on his toes on my behalf."

"A word of caution ..." Whyte moved toward the door. "The admiral is a powerful man but he respects the rules of politics. If the winds change, and playing ball with Swain suits him better, the HCPD could have a bangtail to the *Island Dreamer* in under twelve hours."

"It never hurts to have a friend."

"You find out who the silver lady is and keep an eye on Patti, maybe we can arrange a more permanent station for you."

"That's the cushiest deal I've heard in ages," I said. "You're on."

"I've got to get back to work," he said. "We're docking soon. Stay here as long as you like. They'll announce when you need to get back to your seat and harness up."

"Thanks, Hank." I stared out at the Tigris, feeling small and insignificant. "Send me the details on your wife. A 'gram, her usual haunts. I'll see what I can do."

"Of course," he said. "Enjoy the view. And don't let's be seen together from now on if we don't have to be. "

The neat blue shoulders of his uniform strode off the deck and I was left floating, alone, through the stars.

CHAPTER 10

Docking with the *Island Dreamer* was smoother and more seamless than it had any right to be considering the qualifications and track record of the apelike species conducting the operation. But, as Whyte had so matter-of-factly assured me, they never missed, and it proved true at least once more.

I didn't see Whyte again as I disembarked with the passengers into the huge, ovular docking station inside the cruise ship. Like the hangar on Terra Firma, the docking station failed to impress the majority of guests who filed obediently over the designated scaffolding and walkways to reach the exit sign at the far end. I took in the room with my jaw gaping like a virgin at her first peep show.

The docking station was like the inside of a silver egg, webbed with complex support beams and cables that, from my insectile perspective, looked like some kind of glittering alien goo strung from surface to surface. My boots clanged over a metal walkway not unlike the fire escape I'd thrown myself from behind the techRose nightclub. Fortunately, this one appeared to be attached at both ends. I dared myself to look down. More webbed beams and cables and a depth of space I hadn't experienced outside the viewing deck aboard the bangtail. Never mind. I'd just look straight ahead.

As we exited the docking station, the crisp powder-blue suits of *Island Dreamer* crew members met the passengers with holomap downloads and access codes for their assigned rooms and the features they'd shelled out for. Lucky Bastard had spared no expense with my winning ticket. Overwhelmed with the sheer volume of experience packages to choose from, I asked one of the staff members to send the selection to the screen in my room. I loaded the map as an augmentation to my visilens glasses and followed the soft pink glow of arrows superimposed over the labyrinthine passages.

The guest quarters on the *Island Dreamer* appeared to all be located within a honeycomb of suites and hallways on one level. According to the scaled out version of my holomap, the other attractions were scattered across various entertainment floors throughout the cruiser. At first, the corridors echoed with excited voices and reflections of multi-coloured clothing and faces, but as I continued along the path of glowing arrows, I shared the halls with fewer and fewer guests. The map led me on a zigzagging course that seemed to take me, eventually, to the other side of the ship where nothing but silence accompanied me.

The pink arrows ended in a pulsing bullseye pattern similar to the taxi rings next to the HoloCity grid. The outer edge of the circle shrank and moved in toward the centre and a new ring appeared on the outside as if guiding me to stand in the centre. I looked around the empty corridors. The circle was planted directly in front of a wide expanse of seamless white walls. No signage marred the minimalist landscape, and therefore no sign that I was in the wrong place jumped out at me. Other than the fact that there was nothing there. With no other bright ideas, I followed the map onto the circle.

A door materialized in the white wall the moment I had both feet within the circle, and beyond it was a small closet-like room, also empty. The pink arrow flashed for me to enter the box. Again, I followed, and the door closed behind me without a sound. Cold sweat broke out on my forehead, and I spun around inside the empty white cube. I touched the wall where the door had been and felt the faint tingle of electromagnetic feedback from a screen. It wasn't really there, like Hammett's piggy skin, the wall was a hologram projected from a field of nanoparticles with biosensory feedback enhancements enabled. I wondered how many invisible doors were hiding inside the seemingly empty corridors outside.

A soft chime sounded from somewhere above my head and a holographic keypad hovered in front of my face, prompting me for one of the access codes I'd gotten from the *Island Dreamer* crew. I flicked through until I found the right one and keyed it in. The box lifted into the soles of my boots as I was carried smoothly upward to another level. Another chime sounded and the wall in front of me disappeared. I stepped out into a modest bedroom suite, not much bigger than a Trade Baron's palace and stuffed to the rafters with enough Lucky Bastard hooch to keep his brothel in high spirits for a few hours.

When I turned to look behind me, the door had already disappeared into an expanse of pearlescent pink wall. Somewhere on the other side of the room, or maybe it was in the next county, a bed surrounded by a gauzy pink curtain sat. It looked to be patiently awaiting some kind of erotic circus event by the size of it. I dropped my things on a chair that may or may not have been for sitting on and moved toward the centre of the room where a hologuide in the same powder-blue as the rest of the *Island Dreamer* crew wore was standing with his hands clasped daintily in front of him.

"Welcome to you quarters, Ms. Marlowe," the guide said primly. "And congratulations on winning the Lucky Bastard Sweepstakes. You are standing in one of the most prestigious suites available on the luxury cruiser *Island Dreamer*. I will be your guide for the duration of your stay with us, unless you would prefer to transfer a personal smart guide to our system. Would you like a tour of your rooms?"

The hologram had a smarmy old money face, like that of a

servant whose family has been in service to royalty for so long he's beginning to think he's royal himself. I scanned the other available guide skins and grimaced. Even with Lucky Bastard springing for the pay-to-play options, the list was a worst-of compilation of cush-drunk classics. With such gems as Immigrant House-Boy with Python in Banana Hammock, and Gravity Defying Knockers on Trampoline, even the greasy butler wasn't looking too bad.

"Do SmartPets work?"

The guide's response took a fraction of a second too long, as if it had to search the archives for an answer to my question. Who goes for Mittens the Menace when they can have Gravity Defying Knockers? The hologuide's bland eyes stared awkwardly in the direction of my face while the invisible gears cranked away. When he blinked back to life he said, "Any personal smart holo device with the most recent security updates installed may be transferred."

"Send me the instructions," I said. "And then blink off."

The guide looked like he wanted to say something else but his coding prevented him from being rude to a guest. I was imagining it, of course. The *Island Dreamer* wouldn't allow programming with attitude. At least not in a default skin. The House-Boy might give you a little lip if you paid for the service.

I read the directions for transfer and used my tattler to check the status of Hammett's updates. If I prioritized the security updates and ignored the general maintenance ones I could have it up and running in half an hour. I made the changes to the settings and then did some analog exploration of my new digs.

The first thing to catch my attention was a big, silver button glowing gently on the wall opposite where I came into the room. The wall was otherwise unadorned so the button must do something spectacular. Unleash an army of PornoPops maybe, or open onto my own personal buffet of international delicacies. That would be better. I was starving. Either space travel was hard on the equipment or my body sensed the wealth and splendour of my environment and was starting to get ideas about things like nutrition beyond NRG drinks and greasy street cart sausages.

I punched it, hoping now for that dream buffet, and when the wall opened I was a little disappointed. No food. Just the vast, black emptiness of space. The Lucky Bastard suite came quipped with its own personal viewing bubble. Oh well, once Hammett was up and running we could go snuffling for truffles. This heap of space junk probably had a restaurant or two-hundred.

I stepped into the bubble with the same sense of vertigo as I'd had on the deck of the bangtail, but as I stood there, staring out in the vast emptiness of space, the feeling slowly dissolved into a sense of awe. Each glittering dot a star, a nebula, a galaxy. Maybe other planets. It wasn't empty at all, really. It only seemed that way because we were so infinitesimally small in comparison, like atomic fleas. I leaned out from the bubble and tried to see the side of the ship, but all I could see was a glittering wall stretching in all directions. I stood there until my feet started to go numb. I was a flea on a flea.

"Marlowe?" Hammett's voice came from far away. "Where am I?"

I turned my back on cosmic dread and scanned the room. No sign of the pig. "Good morning, sunshine!"

"It's dark in here," it said. "I can't see a thing."

"Sorry, Ham," I said, looking under the bed. "My tattler connected with the base unit automatically, but I didn't actually look to see where it was located."

"I supposed I should be grateful." It sounded anything but. "I expected to come to in a hockmarket chop shop."

"I'm fine, Hammett." I brought up the holomap and swung through endless menus trying to find the map of the room itself. Maybe I should have let the butler give me a tour after all. "Thanks for your concern."

"I don't want to tell you how to do your job—" Hammett said.

"Please do," I said. "While you're at it can you access the room schematics and tell me where you are?"

"Ask it yourself," Hammett said. "I don't have access until you finish the transfer."

"Oh." I asked the room—the cush set have all the fun toys—and found Hammett in the VacBot closet. It trotted out in a powder-blue uniform jacket and a crisp little hat perched between its piggy ears. "Not you, too."

"Do you like it?" Hammett spun for me, corkscrew tail wagging. "Complimentary uniform."

"Half of one, anyway." I reached down and patted it on the bare bum. "Good to see you Hammett."

"I was going to say that you should really try not to poke Swain in the eye next time," Hammett said, staring around the room in cartoon eyed awe. "But it seems to be working pretty well for you so far."

"You think this is cool?" I ticked the last couple of boxes to complete the transfer process and led Hammett to the stargazing deck. "Check out the view."

"Wow. I've always wanted to see the stars." The holoskin flickered as it stepped into the bubble and stared out into space. Its piggy ears twitched. It craned its neck way out to look at the grey expanse of the *Island Dreamer*'s hull. "What's that?"

I climbed into the viewing bubble too and gazed down the length of the cruiser. A hatch had opened in the side of the ship that wasn't there before, and something shiny cartwheeled lazily toward us along the side of hull. "This isn't good."

"It looks like a—" Hammett squinted its eyes at the thing.

My scalp prickled. "It's the woman in the silver dress."

Hammett snorted. "Where's the rest of her?"

I ran a hand through my hair and leaned against the hard, clear plastic of the viewing bubble. The headless corpse bounced off the side of the hull and spun awkwardly away from the ship. The exposed skin was slightly swollen with a skim of frost to match the shiny silver cocktail dress. "Probably wherever she left her necklace."

CHAPTER 11

I ran through the snaking corridors with my visilens glasses guiding me and Hammett trotting importantly at my side. The pig elicited a few of squeals of delight from cross-eyed co-eds stumbling off the entertainment deck but otherwise no one paid any attention to us. I attempted to get patched through to Whyte with no success and the holomap kept all the crew-and-employee-only areas locked behind access codes. Apparently, neither Whyte nor the admiral had seen fit to give me a direct line of communication. Don't call us, we'll call you.

I hopped on a transport pod and sped toward the central security unit. I was pretty sure Hollard and Whyte would be unenthused if I started screaming about headless women floating past my viewing deck, so I put on my "I'd-like-to-speak-with-the-manager" face and got ready to accost the first powder-blue suit I saw.

As I cruised along in the self-driving pod, I scanned the crowds. The entertainment deck swarmed with cush-drunk wardrobe choices that looked like they'd been summoned directly from a surrealist nightmare. Holoskin enhancements replaced the physical kind among the high-fashion set—men with bull's heads and women with tails, towering androgynous creatures with iridescent scales. Oh my.

Groups of Last Humanist acolytes glided serenely through the chaos with their pink robes flowing behind them like the burbling waters of a psychedelic stream. I kept my head down and avoided them at all costs. I'd had enough culty weirdness for one day. My techhead buddies, and anyone who looked like them, were absent from the party, much to the relief of the acolytes, I was sure. I wondered if they'd gotten a refund before or after the sadistic security officers scraped their insides off the red-tube-of-death.

"You know," Hammett said, standing up on the seat with its hooves pressed against the backrest, "You're a little underdressed for this crowd."

"Someone in this crowd has just relieved a woman of her head and jettisoned her corpse into the wild black yonder."

"You might want to try to fit in, then."

"I might not."

"Does the new arm have a nanoparticle field?" The pig wiggled its tail at me. "You could turn it into a gorilla fist or something. Animal skins are very 'in' right now."

"I have no idea, Ham." I said. "I didn't have time to get the rundown from Rae. It grabs and punches. That's all I really need."

"Send me the manual."

I tried to access the prototype's documentation. Nothing. I pushed a button and a long, thin blade popped out of my index finger. "Whoops."

"Be careful with that thing!" Hammett squealed. "You could have shot me."

"Nah," I said, and bent the curved blade with my other finger. "No firearms. Rae knows me too well for that. Security was tight, besides. I'd never have gotten on board with guns in my guns. This blade is pretty flimsy or they probably would have nailed me for it, too. What's with this thing?"

"It looks like a grapefruit knife."

"Who the hell can afford grapefruit?"

"The same kind of people who can afford a prosthetic like that." The pig looked meaningfully at the crowd. "And probably every single person on this ship besides you."

I pushed the button again and the blade retracted. "I'll have to ping Rae and get the scoop. Until then—"

"It grabs and it punches." Hammett rolled its eyes. "You're such a Neanderthal."

"Speaking of which," I said, pointing out a group of acolytes cutting through the swath of inebriated tech addicts, "what do you figure the Last Humanists are doing aboard a luxury space cruise?"

The pig yawned, a bit rich coming from a fully charged robot. "Conversion units. What else?"

"Am I boring you?" I hit the kill switch on the transport pod when the glowing blue dome of the security station loomed into view. "I could have left you at home."

"Don't get sore," Hammett said and hopped out of the pod. "The pinkies are just about the least interesting thing in this place."

"What interests me is why silver dresses seem to carry a death sentences these days."

"How about those necklaces everyone is wearing? Why don't you have one of those?"

I whipped my head around. The pig was right. At least half of the women and some of the men all wore the same necklace. A silver choker with a teardrop pendant glittering at their throats, some clear. Some as red as blood. I winced as my P.I. instincts pounded into a chrome wall. Must have been taking a back-alley piss on that one.

"For a Grit District pro skirt, it's worth your life to wear a piece like that," I said. "Up here looks like it's just another high-cush-low-substance uniform for the fashion fascists."

Was that all they were?

Hammett trotted toward the security station with its tail held high. "Well, I think they look nice. It wouldn't hurt you to try to fit in a little more."

The crowd swelled and moved around us in waves. A group of girls all sporting the red pendants scanned the party goers coyly. I watched as one by one they dissolved into the sea of people. It was tough to track them in the chaos of glitter and chrome of the entertainment deck, but one girl with a tall stack of bright yellow curls stood out above the crowd. She pulled someone into a rounded cubby cut into the white skin of the ship's interior, running her hands up and down his arms as expertly as any pro skirt at techRose. But whatever she was selling the punter didn't want it, because he slipped back into the crowd without so much as a wave goodbye. Maybe he had her room number. Then the girl spilled out into the rush with her eyes bright and her hair electric.

And the red pendant looked anemic under the bright lights.

I chewed on that for a while. Why did the necklaces change colour? Is this how Blanco was moving the Tropical Punch? We snaked our way through the bazaar toward the security dome which shimmered like an oasis at the end of the strip. "Since when do you care about my fashion choices?"

"Since I have to be seen in public with you." The pig gave me a scathing sidelong glance.

"To market, to market, to hock a fat pig ..."

Hammett smiled sweetly up at me with little throbbing hearts in place of its pupils. It batted its eyelashes. "You look fabulous in that jumpsuit, darling."

"That's better." I said, but my jaw tightened around the playful banter I usually enjoyed with my oldest, truest friend.

The security dome rose out of the crowd like an alien moon rising from a sea glittering with high-fashion phytoplankton. The other passengers avoided it, so the crush of bodies seemed to swell and crash on its celestial shores. Even in the cush set, nobody liked security unless they were in trouble. Serious trouble, or it's not worth the risk of their contraband drugs and illicit tech being sniffed out by an overzealous lawman.

As we approached, the club district gave way to holographic palm trees and an expanse of white sand beaches that hadn't been visible from the transport car. The crowd thinned until we stood like the lone survivors of a shipwreck on a deserted shoreline. We stepped through an invisible barrier and the crowd and all the noise that went with it disappeared so that it was just us and the glowing blue dome.

"Neat trick," Hammett said, trotting ahead, its holographic hooves leaving little heart-shaped prints in the holographic sand. "You don't see holotech like this in the city."

"What do you know?" Artificial light beamed down on me from above, and I wiped authentic sweat from my brow with the back of my hand. "You've spent your entire existence in my apartment."

"Don't remind me." Hammett glared over its shoulder at me. "Luckily, I have feed access so I can keep up to date on all the things I've been missing out on."

"Don't they want to be able to see out there?" I bent down and scooped up a handful of sand. It was warm and glittered with bits of mica as I let it spill out between my fingers. If I didn't know better, I'd have bet a fat stack of cred that it was real. "Keep an eye on things?"

"They probably can," Hammett said. "But it gives visitors the impression that they are completely alone. Makes them more inclined to talk."

"Monkey psychology." I trudged toward the dome. "Silky."

"Simple and effective." Hammett trotted along beside me. "Humans really aren't as complex as they think they are."

"A human created you."

It grinned. "And an AI improved me."

"The humans created the AI too." The simulated sunshine was giving me a headache. The dome glowed too brightly against the sand.

"Sure," Hammett said. "And then it improved itself."

"So you're better than me now?"

"The purpose of artificial intelligence is to be more powerful than its organic forebear," Hammett said. "Did I hurt your feelings?"

"If you ever do, I'll just unplug you."

Hammett's smile drooped. "Neanderthal."

I pushed open the door to security, and a grim-faced woman with an olive complexion and coal-black hair tucked neatly under her white cap looked up from her desk.

"*Island Dreamer* security." Her voice was carefully neutral, and she shuffled through the papers on her desk. She eyed my pink metal arm and then bared her teeth in an approximation of friendliness. "How can I help you?"

"I need to speak with your Captain of Security."

She kept the filmy smile plastered on her face. "Can I see the papers on your cyber enhancement, please?"

"I've already been through your scanner." I clenched my fists and took a deep breath. "I need to speak with Whyte."

"Standard procedure, ma'am." She tapped the edge of a stack of papers on the desk and kept smiling. "The ticket of manufacture and your proof of ownership will do."

"This is an emergency."

"You can make an emergency call from your room or from your own communication device by using the S.O.S commands provided to you upon your arrival."

I leaned on the desk separating us and glared down at her. "If you don't get Whyte for me, you're going to be making an emergency call of your own."

The woman's hand crept under the desk where I imagined she was about to push a button that did exactly that.

"Marlowe," Hammett whispered up at me. "Just show the

officer your papers and get on with it."

I resisted the urge to punt the pig into the wall, but the woman behind the desk looked at me sharply. "You're Bubbles Marlowe?"

"Yes," I said. "And I want to talk to Whyte or the admiral is going to hear about it."

The colour blanched from her tanned skin, leaving behind a sallow shadow of her complexion. "Apologies, ma'am. I'll patch him in."

A door into the back room opened, and Whyte stepped out with an unlit cigar dangling from his lip. Sweat beaded across the tanned leather of his forehead. He gritted his teeth in a way that might have been mistaken for a smile in a funhouse mirror. "That won't be necessary."

I whirled to face him. "You've just been hiding back there while she had me on the hotplate?"

"What do you want?" He chewed on the end of the black stick. "Is your room not to you liking? I don't want—"

"The room is fine," I growled. "It's what just floated past my view that has me a little concerned."

Whyte narrowed his cold-blue peepers at me until they disappeared in a burst of wrinkles. "I'm not in the mood for mind games, Marlowe."

"You want me to jump on the desk and scream about it, or should we find somewhere quiet to talk? We have a serious problem."

Whyte spun on his heel and stalked back into the room he came out of. I gave the woman behind the desk a look that dared her to say something and then I followed him. Hammett made it all the way to the door, and was about to step inside the room when the pig stopped, twirled once, and sat on its haunches. "I'll wait here."

"It's a quiet room," Whyte said. "No outside bots. You'll have to exercise your grey matter and remember our conversation on your own."

"It's just a SmartPet." I swung my upgrade in ahead of me and didn't feel any resistance, so I stepped inside and closed the door behind me.

"We take every precaution," he said from behind a grey desk.

I sat myself in a hard grey plastic chair opposite him. The floor under my boots was grey. The walls. The filing cabinets. The only colour in the room was Whyte's crisp navy uniform and his burnt sienna face. No pictures on the wall, no papers on the desk. The room had all the charm of a sensory deprivation unit.

"Not every precaution, apparently." I put my hands on my knees and leaned forward. "Who has access to your cargo ports?"

The wrinkled skin of his sunburned neck strained against the collar of his uniform as he leaned in to meet me, hissing through clenched teeth. "I've got the Last Bloody Humanists ringing in complaints about the relentless assault on their religious freedom.

My wife has just spent a fortune on complementary fashion accessories for the Gold Star guest rooms. I just had to break up a fight between two boutique cosmetics dealers. Comms are misfiring. I have about this much patience for incompetence right now."

He pinched his fingers in front of my face.

"So I've still got a little wiggle room."

"What is this about, Marlowe? I was told that you would be an independent contractor. I don't have time to babysit. That's why I hired you in the first place. So what is it? The admiral's job or my wife?"

"I don't know," I said. "Is your wife in the habit separating good-time girls from their thinking units?"

The bluster oozed out of him like stale air from an old balloon. Whyte sagged into his chair. "What? The girl can't be dead already."

"Maybe not," I said. "But a corpse in a cute silver number floated past my viewing deck about half an hour ago minus the complicated bits. So if you've got an eye on the admiral's girl we should probably take a peek. And regardless of who the lucky vetch was, we should take a look at a list of the crew who has access to those ports."

Whyte closed his eyes. "You should have called me directly."

"You think I didn't try that?" I thumped his desk with my upgrade and left a dent in the flawless grey surface. "I don't have access to you or the admiral from my tattler and the room has you both flagged as unlisted."

Whyte's eyes snapped open and he barked a command that brought up a holoscreen between us. He flipped through a bunch of menus faster than I could follow and scanned a long list of names and numbers until he stopped on Betty Marlowe, Lucky Bastard. He tapped my name. Nothing happened. He tapped it again. He said, "Show me your tattler."

I tried to bring up his name on my tattler and showed him the fuzzed out exchange link.

His teeth ground right through the end of his stogie, and the black stick fell onto his desk with a spray of tobacco so dark you'd think it had already been smoked. He spat the stub onto the floor. No scrubber bot appeared to clean it up. "I don't believe this."

"I've got an extra piece of gum if you want."

"You're being blocked." The words hissed out between tightly clamped teeth. "The admiral is going to be furious."

"So you didn't forget to add me to your buddy list?" I sat back, feeling slightly less annoyed at the situation. "Here I thought I just didn't rate in your books."

"It shouldn't be possible."

"That's what I thought," I said. "I'm a delight."

"We have the best security money can buy," he snapped. "The admiral spares no expense."

"You have the best security legitimate money can buy." I flexed the fingers on my upgrade. "Black-market hackers are always a step ahead of their marks."

"We should have caught it." The tendons in his neck worked as he attempted to swallow the news. "We have the best—"

"You're going to catch it if the admiral finds out," I said. "Now that you know, maybe you can run some counter spyware and find the cracks in your armour. See if you can get a lock on the silver lady, or her last known location. The body was jettisoned from the same side of the ship as my viewing deck. If your cameras are working we should be able to see who gave her the long goodbye."

Whyte scowled at me. His deep voice rumbled in his chest as he said, "I know how to do my job, Marlowe."

"Don't mind me." I raised my hands up and leaned back in the chair. I spoke to the grey ceiling. "I'm just the help."

Whyte did some cursing and swiped furiously through the holoscreen windows. I stared at the uniform cracks between the tiles of the ceiling. A tiny, black fly flicked its wings and crawled toward the overhead light in a zombified stupor. You can take a fly into outer space and it's still just a fly, mindlessly buzzing for the light. And humans are just apes in funny suits.

My tattler pinged and I looked down to see a notification from Whyte. I flicked open a file on his wife. "You got through."

"I told you, I know how to do my job."

Patti Whyte was everything her husband had described, and more. Smooth brown skin like polished marble, and a thick

131

cascade of mahogany curls down her back. She had full purple lips and eyes as sharp as tacks. Whyte, with his smoked-meat complexion and dried out husk of a personality, didn't rate for half a wife like that. Unless the security gig was more lucrative in the luxury space cruise sector than it was anywhere else—which, I supposed, it had every right to be. My eyes flicked to Whyte through the 'gram. Was he seeing what I was seeing? No, he just saw his wife. I saw an almost exact duplicate of the girl in the silver dress. Different hair. Different makeup. Same build, though. Same look in her eyes. Patti stared at me out of the 'gram like she was daring me to guess her secrets. I made her a promise and killed the 'gram.

"Find anything on the pro skirt?" I looked up at Whyte

He looked back at me with the blank look of someone working on a difficult puzzle, then he brought up a live feed of a laughing woman in a low cut silver dress. A choker-style necklace with a ruby tear glittered in her clavicle. "Game Room Twelve, Fortunes' Favour, at the roulette wheel."

I brought up the original 'gram of my girl from the mystery client and compared the two. Like Patti, she had the same petite build and the vaguely familiar look of all people who wear too much makeup. She could be the same woman as the one I found in techRose who had no sister but managed to do the twin show with another woman with the right build in the right dress and makeup. She could be the same woman, or she could be someone else entirely. Either my client had neglected to mention that her sister was a triplet, or something else was going on.

"They're decoys."

"For what?"

"No missing persons reported yet?" I called up a map to Fortune's Favour and sent it to the visilenses. "I'm going to check on our silver lady. I want to see her with my own eyes."

"The feed is secure." Whyte flexed his jaw at me a couple of times. "You're sure you saw what you think you saw?"

"I haven't been hitting the Lucky Bastard if that's what you're asking." I stood abruptly and sent the fly buzzing. "Speaking of which, can someone relieve me of the gin-splosion happening in my room right now? I haven't been sober for so long that I feel the need to prove it to myself or anyone else."

He stood up to walk me to the door. "We'll keep an eye on the girl. I want you to watch Patti."

"Rendezvous at 1900 hours tomorrow," I said. "I got it."

"Maybe it wouldn't hurt to find her before then so you can—"

"You know how to do your job, Hank. I know how to do mine."

"Fine. I'll check the footage from the cargo docks. Try to keep it low key."

I opened the door and bent to pat Hammett on the head. The nanoparticle field tickled my fingers. Then it tickled my brain. My cheek muscles smiled on autopilot. I said, "I don't know any other way to play."

I left the security dome with Hammett prancing along beside me in the sand. Instead of following the holomap toward the game rooms, I pulled up a different list. A pattern itched at the edge of my consciousness, but a thread was tugging them together now, as thin and red as a plasma wire. I needed a bathing suit. Despite what I'd told Whyte, it might be time to hit the holobeaches and see if I could run into Mrs. Hank Whyte a little ahead of schedule.

CHAPTER 12

Upon Hammett's enthusiastic recommendation I dropped all of my Lucky Bastard retail credits on a deconstructed wetsuit that looked more like go-go boots and short shorts than swimwear to my stylistically challenged eye. As much as I hated to admit it, my porky companion knew the glad-rag landscape. In the beach district, I blended in like a diaphanous blob in the effulgence of ultra-modern swim sophistication.

"Shouldn't we be prioritizing the admiral's case?" Hammett snuffled around in the vicinity of my toes, inspecting the spray of sand along the imitation boardwalk. "I mean, I'd love to see the beach but this isn't really the time—"

"I am prioritizing the admiral's case." I blinked my eyes up at the massive neon signs advertising doors to various virtual aquatic experiences—Lonely Lagoon, White Sands of Paradise, 80th Moon of Jupiter, Glacial Runoff, Relaxing Reefs. "But there are too many coincidences lining up here and I don't like coincidences. I'm going to pay a visit to Patti Whyte and pick her brain."

The scent of sun-warmed skin, tanning oils, and salt water wafted out of the air-circulation system with hints of melted ice cream and burnt street cart hot dogs—artificial sensory triggers from a time lost to memory but which evoked a bizarre sense of residual nostalgia. I'd never been to the time or place these scenes were from and yet it was familiar as a dream. I puzzled over the possibility of genetic memory until I realized the sensation itself was another neurochemical stimulation. These cush pushers have all the fun. The farther off the glam path I trudged, the stronger the feeling became, until I turned to a collection of back-alley sims labelled as "Memory Lane."

I tracked Whyte's wife to a lesser-used sim with a shabby driftwood sign painted with a young woman on a flotation device and "Amity Island Welcomes You" in peeling blue letters. As if as an afterthought, someone had scrawled a rough, black triangle poking out of the water beside the girl.

"Are you sure this is the right place?" Hammett whispered up at me. It sniffed the air cautiously.

"He's managed to get a tracker on her," I said and grabbed a towel from a faded rainbow of cotton terry fabric crammed haphazardly onto a sun-bleached wooden shelf leaning against the wall. "All I have to do is follow the pretty lights."

Hammett sniffed at the entrance to the Amity Beach simulation and said, "I can't go in there."

"Can you drop the skin?" I picked the pig up and set it on the towel shelf. "Watch the crowd for me."

Hammett disappeared, leaving a smooth metallic sphere in its place. The sphere reflected the colour of the towels, so that in most directions it blended in seamlessly with the shelf. Not that there was anyone else in Memory Lane to worry about. The scent of sunscreen and nostalgia was for me alone. The SmartPet made a blip inside my ear tubes that only I could hear. "There is no crowd."

"I'll be back soon."

"This is discrimination, you know." The pig snorted even without its little pink nose. "I'm filing a complaint."

"Thanks, Ham."

I glanced over my shoulder just as a trio of Last Humanist acolytes entered "Memory Lane." They scanned the empty corridor with their faces set in eerie facsimiles of benign curiosity. But their eyes hardened when they passed over me. Cold disapproval radiated from the group as they paused, then turned back the way they came.

I waited until they were out of sight, then slipped through the holoscreen separating Amity Beach from the corridor outside and stepped into another world. I stood in a flat concrete parking area with old-fashioned gas burning cars packed in like the canned, meat-free sausages they always have for sale in the Grit District. A gentle sea breeze carried cries of white gulls as they soared across blue skies like a choreographed kite display. Rays of intense sunlight beat down and burrowed into my exposed flesh like burning worms. The asphalt radiated the heat back up at me with an oily petroleum burn in it.

I grabbed a discarded bottle of sunscreen sitting on the concrete barrier between the parking lot and the beach and sluiced some hot, greasy lotion into the palm of my hand marvelling at the way the white liquid slid across my skin. Some people like the sun-exposed look, and I knew there were simulation units that used actual radiation to complete the experience for their customers. I hoped that using the lotion would signal to the algorithms that I didn't want any roasting today. Judging by the leathery hides crawling around on the beach the de rigueur look for this particular beach set was "well-done."

Inside the simulation, my visilenses no longer gave me a signal on Patti Whyte's location. Hundreds of bodies swarmed over the beach. Patti preferred the sentimental flesh pollution of traditional Old Earth public beaches where every square inch of synthetic sand was packed with oversized bottoms spilling out of undersized triangles of fabric. In my deconstructed wetsuit, I stood out like a thumb dipped in molten platinum. The beach goers ignored me. If there were any other real people in here other than Patti, and judging by the hollowness of Memory Lane there weren't, they likely had their settings tuned to scene blending. That way any foreign intrusion into the aesthetic landscape would be adjusted by the simulation in order not to disrupt the fantasy.

"Can you still hear me, Hammett?"

The speakers in my ear tubes crackled and the pig's voice came through as if from the bottom of a well, full of echoes and static. "Barely. There's something blocking the comms here, like at Whyte's office, but stronger."

"Hang tight. She's got to be here."

I shoved my way into the throng and moved toward the water. Children screamed and parents scolded. Teenagers shrieked and giggled and chased one another across the sand, careless of whom they sprayed with cold water and wet sand. Bits of silica stuck to my skin where I had applied the lotion, and I longed to escape the crowd of people by diving under the crystalline waves of the wide blue ocean just visible above the sandy mops of hair ahead. But when I got to the shoreline, the pristine waters of the horizon were torn apart by thrashing limbs and the joyous squawking of sunburned primates.

At the edge of the chaos, something else moved through the water. A slick black blade cut through the waves like a knife paring away the outer flesh as it sliced closer and closer to the core. The simulated crowd hadn't noticed the threat yet. I stood on the wet sand with waves crashing over my boots and cold water seeping between my toes with my eyes on that blade as it swept—back and forth, back and forth—toward a young boy floating on a raft just a little too far from the crowd.

The muscles in my chest tightened. The part of my brain that knew it was floating through outer space on a luxury cruiser, hundreds of kilometres above Terra Firma and far from the threat of oceanic predators, was a tiny inconsequential thing in the face of the screaming panic of the monkey brain. My eyes were glued to the black blade and the little boy. When the blade slipped under the waves I couldn't tear my eyes from the expanse of glittering water ahead of the boy, so deathly calm.

"Beautiful isn't it?"

A woman in a wide brimmed black hat appeared next to me. A funereal veil fluttered about her face in the breeze, black lace embellished cheerfully with polka dots. Beneath the veil, large black sunglasses hid her eyes from me. I said, "Patti?"

A primal scream tore through the air from somewhere in the mass of swimmers and suddenly everyone was dragging at one another, trying to get their own fleshy bodies to shore before anyone else. Other cries rose out of the water, piercing the splashing of waves and the screeching of gulls. The kind of noises that rake through your brain and turn off all other inputs. Panic. Escape. Sunburned flesh thrashed and crashed in the white foam and chunks of flying sand and seaweeds.

As each swimmer made it to shore they blinked out of existence. The beach behind us stretched on infinitely, a desert planet of endless swirling dunes and hot dry air blasting sand at my face. Eddies of star-strewn indigo hung with huge purple and pink moons replaced the sun-shining skies. The screams stopped.

"If you're here," Patti said. "It may already be too late."

I looked back out onto the water where a glassy twilit surface reflected the berry hues of the galaxy kissed sky. Tiny waves lapped at the soft pink sands of the desert beach, kissing gently. The black blade sliced back and forth smoothly, parallel to the shore.

"I'm here," I said. "But where are you?"

"I can't tell you that." She pulled the hat off, pinching the brim between her fingers and tossing the hat into the water where it sunk slowly beneath the glassy surface. Her mahogany hair appeared black in the strange light. Her pale skin was darkened by the simulation. She wore a silver choker at her neck with a pendant, like a drop of blood, at her throat.

"Your husband is worried about you."

She smiled sadly, looking more and more like the girl in the silver dress. "I never meant to hurt Hank. He's a good man."

"I can help you," I said. "Whatever this mess is, we can get you out of it."

"You can help me," she said. "But not in the way that you think."

"I'm not taking any more falls for you."

"I'm sorry for techRose. I tried to warn you. There was nothing you could do, but I had hoped—Jimi trusted you, so I thought—"

A nerve in my stump fired off for no reasons and my index finger twitched. "Jimi?"

"He's dead because of me. They're all dying because of me."

"Who is dying?"

The Pattie Whyte simulation took a step into the waves. Her black dress fell off of her shoulders revealing a skin of glittering silver beneath. "I work for the Rose."

"You husband thinks you work for Libra."

The simulation flickered. "So does Libra. I'm a scientist."

"What does the Rose have to do with anything? Why are the Last Humanists on board the *Island Dreamer*? Did you bring them here?"

"We believe in the Absolute Purity of the Human Form. That does not stop us from enjoying the advancements of science."

"This simulation," I said. "Is this you in your purest form?"

The woman froze. Then she said, "I can only answer the questions that Patti Whyte anticipated you would ask."

"Okay, so tell me what a Libra scientist is doing working for an anti-tech cult."

"The Last Humanists fund medical research that focuses on advancing human biology without the use of technological contaminants."

"How noble," I said. "I look forward to receiving a new arm."

"Re-growing limbs is too slow and expensive, yet, to be a viable solution to the average HoloCity citizen. We do not begrudge you the use of your enhancement."

I bent to pick up a piece of seaweed from the foamy surf and coiled the cold, wet leaves around my real fingers. "Noble and generous."

"I was there," she said. "When you stopped Whip Tesla from selling those vials. I ran. I couldn't afford to be caught—"

"Whip Tesla was selling to a man." I strained my fingers against the seaweed until the rubbery material snapped and fell from my hand. "To a guy named Punch Blanco. Maybe you've heard of him."

"Punch Blanco doesn't exist."

"I saw him with my own eyes. It's my description of him that they put on the police bulletin."

"You are seeing this beach with your own eyes."

"You're telling me what, that Punch Blanco was a skin? HCPD has scanners built into all patrol helmets. We'd have seen right through it. Punch Blanco is as real as I am, and I got my arm blown off to prove it."

"It probably won't surprise you to learn that the HCPD is not using the latest technology. In fact, Chief Swain skims as much as he can off of the surveillance and PPE budget as he can get away with."

That information rated with my experience of the department. "Figures."

"Swain is the hand behind a cartel of black-market drug and tech syndicates that run the Grit District. Your accident had nothing to do with the drug bust and everything to do with Swain's remarkable sense of self-preservation."

"Have you ever met Swain?" My lip curled involuntarily. "He's not exactly Libra material."

"Swain isn't clever, but he has excellent survival instincts. He understands power and influence and he knows how to play to his strengths."

"What's he worried about Blanco for, then?"

"Someone is targeting syndicate customers." She stared at the black fin and wet her lips with the tip of her small pink tongue. "Swain's failure to protect them is making him look weak."

"And letting Whip Tesla go was supposed to help that image? No. It doesn't add up."

"Tesla was ours. He was supposed to make a delivery to a Last Humanist operative, a new nootropic drug my team at Libra has been working on for years. A mind expanding drug that could blow open the limits of human consciousness, without relying on virtual realities or technological stimulation of the brain. This drug will force the evolution of the human species if used correctly."

"The Last Humanists are about to burst out of the human chrysalis, and you hire thugs like Tesla?

"Lower human forms have their uses." The simulation smiled benignly. "They come with the advantage of easy to read manuals and controls. But if handled incorrectly they can be exceedingly frustrating. True logic defies the dregs, and their behaviour becomes difficult to predict."

I wondered if Patti had forgotten she was still a human too. Whether she'd partaken of this magical new drug or not. I said, "And where do I rate on this hierarchy of humanity?"

The Patti sim ignored me. "Tesla planned to double cross us and sell the drug to one of Swain's pin men. I wasn't able to get secure communication to the Rose in time to stop the delivery so I used a skin of my own design to attempt to intercept it. I failed."

"And Swain relieved Tesla of the goods, claimed it was a dud batch, and passed it on to the pin and pinchers."

"This drug wasn't meant for the masses. It was designed only for those of Absolute Purity."

"Is that why the pinches are turning up dead?" I took out a piece of gum and stared at it without putting it into my mouth. The pink waves smelled like bubble gum. "The ship is buzzing about Blanco being on the *Island Dreamer*, they're practically lining up to get hammered by Tropical Punch. Convenient that ship security screened out all the passengers with internal implants. It looks to me like the perfect set up for getting a bunch of high-cush wastrels addicted to a new designer drug. If I didn't know better I'd think it was being transported inside those necklaces everyone is wearing."

The simulation froze and flickered again. "Everyone? There is only one necklace that matters."

"Bubbles?" Hammett's voice crackled in my ear tubes.

"Someth—...out...—ere..."

Whatever it was would have to wait. This was probably the only chance I'd get to pump the Patti sim for information.

"Okay, so you say Jimi Ng was on your team. I don't think so. That kid had more upgrades than a cushy VR gaming system. He had 'better living through technology' tattooed on his left ass cheek. He wouldn't have anything to do with the Last Humanist racket. You're going to have to do better than that."

"Jimi had no idea who he worked for."

"So why did he die?"

The beach closed in around us like a horseshoe of pink sand, with palm trees fluttering in a breeze I could no longer feel. A single crescent moon hung above the bay now, a thin white sliver, its reflection scattered over the surface of the ocean like fingernail clippings. The black fin circled the bay as if it was waiting for something.

"Jimi discovered an antidote to the fatal formula, only days after I had passed on the first sample batch to Tesla for delivery to the Mezzanine. But he—" The simulation flickered and I lost what she said.

Hammett crackled in again, sounding pretty nervous for a bundle of wires and microchips. "Bubbles?"

"Not now, Ham," I said into my earpiece. "What's the smoke, Patti? I want to know what happened to Jimi. Exactly what do you think I'm going to be able to do about any of this?"

The woman stood in water with the purple hued waves lapping at her thighs just below the hem of her silver skirt. The black dress she had been wearing slipped beneath the surface like shadowy jellyfish. Her image flickered. Through her diaphanous form I saw the fin turn toward the shore and slip lazily along with the waves in our direction. She blinked out and then reappeared farther down the beach. "I need you to deliver the other formula for me."

"Forget it," I said. "I'm not digging myself into the drug scene any deeper than I've already fallen. I've only got one arm to pull myself out by, remember?"

A sunset had spilled across the horizon like melting strawberry ice cream, frozen in time. The waves flickered back and forth and then stopped. The shark fin disappeared. The woman stood motionless with her arms open to the sun, her silver dress glittering in the strange pink glow. "HoloCity is diseased. I have the cure. Only the Rose can ensure it gets to the people who need it most. I've done all I can."

"The leader of the Last Humanists?" I asked. "Where do I find him?"

Her fingers slipped beneath her long dark hair and unclasped the silver choker. She turned to me with the red teardrop jewel of the pendent glittering in the surreal light. I reached for it and she dropped the necklace into my metal palm. A shock of electricity jolted through my upgrade and into my nerves and the whole simulation blinked out.

I stood in an empty white room with soundproofed walls. A sterile blankness replaced the scents of surf and sand and sunscreen. My head felt hollow as I turned toward the exit. I rotated my metal shoulder and wiggled my fingers.

"Hurry, Bubbles," Hammett's voice appeared, crystal clear and anxious, in my ears. "Security is coming this way, and they don't look happy."

CHAPTER 13

I exited the holobeach, towelling imaginary sand from my suit as if I'd just been swimming. Three guards in powder-blue uniforms waited for me on the deserted Memory Lane boardwalk. "Nice gig you've got here. A girl could get used to the beach life. I could have sworn I had sand all up in my—"

"Bubbles Marlowe?" A tall, blonde security guard stood there, tapping a baton against her palm. She had the body of a prizefighter and a face to match, with a mashed-up nose and quick, mean eyes.

I dropped the towel to the ground and scooped Hammett off the shelf. It popped back into its piggy skin and shook itself like it was trying to get the fit right. I set it on the ground and put my metal hand on my hip. "That's me. Are you the room service? I asked Whyte to get rid of the—"

"You're supposed to be in Game Room Twelve," the woman said. "We've been trying to get a hold of you for the last hour."

"I don't remember signing any paperwork to that effect." I checked my tattler. "Comms are functioning and pings are on. Why didn't you—"

"We've been calling," she snapped. "You've got us blocked."

"You have a nasty habit of interrupting."

Hammett snorted. "Now you know how I feel."

"Not now, pig," I said. "These fine security guards seem to have a problem. It's our job to drop everything and help them, don't you know?"

"Whyte is waiting for you in Fortune's Favour." The guard narrowed her hard green eyes at me. "We'll escort you."

"That rates. It really does. Class service. But I need to get back to my room to change first. I can find my way to the gaming district myself. I'm a big girl. I can read maps and everything."

"You're coming with us." The baton tap-tapped a little faster, like she was getting warmed up.

I sighed and bent down. I picked Hammett off the ground and tucked the towel under my arm. The skin blinked off as I slipped the sphere into my bag and slung it over my shoulder. I said, "Alright."

The towel flew through the air like the money piece in a

high-end strip tease, more style than substance. But it hit the front woman in the head and wrapped around her lumpy face. The two younger guards blinked in confusion as the brains of their operation cursed me with every colourful word she could think of in at least three different languages. In one hand, her baton started to buzz and glowed with an ominous blue light. She grabbed at the towel with her other hand, swinging wildly in front of her in case I was stupid enough to walk into her batting zone.

The guard on her right, a cute number who was still growing pimples in the place of facial hair and whose greasy red hair didn't quite seem up to the admiral's standards, was that stupid. He lunged for me with eyes wide in that I-don't-know-what-to-do-but-I-have-to-do-something brand of panicked determination just as the woman swung back for a mean crack. The young buck took the baton in the throat and dropped, twitching, to the floor. His spasming leg knocked the feet out of the blonde and she went down, too, the charged stick sandwiched between their two bodies in a pile of jerking limbs. The towel was still wrapped around the blonde's noodle, which was too bad. I'd have liked to see the look on her face.

The last man standing was a little, pink-faced guy with a face like a bald lab rat. He looked at the pile of arms and legs and then he looked at me. He hissed, lips pulled back to reveal crooked yellow teeth. His eyes had the kind of eager look that said he enjoyed pain when it was somebody else who was feeling it. I raised my eyebrows and stepped toward him with my upgrade raised. His eyes darted to his fallen comrades. No backup. He spun on his heel and hoofed it down the boardwalk like his mother was calling him home for dinner. I took off in the opposite direction, charging into a mob of beach bums on the main mall like a half-naked diva bat out of HoloHell. Even with the threat of rogue guards nipping at my heels I had to fight the urge to linger in the fog of chemical nostalgia wafting out of the air system.

"What is happening?" Hammett squealed in my earpiece. "I'm being knocked about like a piñata in here. What have you done now?"

"No time to explain, Ham." My legs, arms, and lungs pumped as I slid around a sharp corner, slipping on the silica strewn border of the holobeach strip. "Find me a hole in the wall. I need an old-school scatter."

Hammett sent directions to my visilenses. "I don't think I get enough respect for all the things I do for you."

"Save it." I merged into a wave of people coming off the shopping district with their purchases floating along behind them on complementary mag scooters bots designed to increase the ka-ching of credit flipping by eliminating the old but-I-can't-carry-any-more-bags excuse. "You can chew me out when I'm sure I'm not going to get whacked by a plasma wand."

I slowed my pace and weaved in and out of the lines of giggling showboaters in outfits that weren't fit for anything except maybe an intergalactic-themed masquerade orgy. I swam in a sea of carefully made-up faces, intricate hairstyles in every colour of the nebula, and enough glitter to gag a backdoor bouncer at techRose. Some of the looks flickered as we passed through overhead skin scanners, but no one paid it any mind. Cameras recorded the true faces of the passengers as they burrowed through the ship like drunken dung beetles, rolling along their collection of cushy fashion excretions. Once they passed out of the skin scanner's radius, their luscious looks were back and startflight etiquette forbade the mention of errant body hair, extraneous rolls of flesh, or the exposed genitalia of the occasional skin scan flasher.

Tucked between a shop selling organic performance-enhancement supplements and a liquor shop was a narrow maintenance hallway. Elegant, frosted glass bottles glittered at me as we neared. The swill was priced to drain your bank account as quickly as your liver enzymes, and still I felt the pull of it. I looked away, guiltily.

"You don't really want it," Hammett reminded me. "It's a pattern of memory your brain hasn't forgotten yet. Like the phantom limb."

"I know," I said. "But it feels real."

"Both will fade with time."

Hammett led me into the corridor. I swallowed against the dry mouth and the imagined thirst, and followed. Doors packed neatly down both sides, just big enough to slide past after a good old-fashioned curry house purge. I crept past each one trying the unlock mechanisms and hoping for the best, but they were all sealed up tighter than a—

"Stop!" Hammett squealed into my ear canal. "That one. The

alarm is disabled."

I tried the lock again, but it was a no-go. "You're sure?"

"I would think I'd have earned a little trust from you by this point."

"If you say so." I punched a neat hole through the door with my upgrade and pulled it sideways into the wall. No high-tech holoscreens for the maintenance closets. I slid inside, and closed the door behind me. I was inside a small, dark room that could have been anything from a control station to an emergency toilet for all I could see.

"Now get me out of this bag. It smells like old socks in here."

"You don't have a real nose."

"I have contaminant sensors," it snapped in my ears, and jostled around in the bag. "Which are real enough for me."

I pulled Hammett's sphere out of my back pack and set it on what felt like a countertop or maybe a big metal box. The pig skin popped back into place and the nanoparticles glowed with a slightly bioluminescent sheen as the SmartPet scanned the room. Long, silver bodies hung on the wall, like people made from tubes and spheres, all blank faced and drooping. "What is this place?"

"A supply closet for SmartBots." Hammett shook its skin and stomped its feet in a little dance of frustration. "Tell me what happened. Why did Whyte's guards attack you?"

"Those weren't Whyte's guards." I sat on a metal box and checked my upgrade for damages. "Or if they were, they weren't there on his orders."

"But they said—"

"They said what they thought they should say to get me to come along with them."

Hammett sat on its round, pink haunches, still glowing faintly, and cocked its head at me so that one ear flopped up and the other down. "Humans are so devious. I don't know how your species has survived for so long."

"If you AI types hang around us for long enough, you'll get devious too. It's already hard to tell if you're talking to a person or a well coded program."

"What did Mrs. Whyte have to say?"

"She wasn't there." I brought up my tattler and checked for messages. "Mr. Whyte must have expected as much. He was pretty eager for me to pay her a visit."

I had three missed calls from Detective Tom Weiland, but no message. And a couple of unintelligible texts from Dickie, which reminded me that I had some yelling to do in his direction.

Hammett said. "If she wasn't there, what took you so long?"

"She left a message for me," I said. "I had to get as much as I could out of her ghost before anyone else got wise to it. Which I did, just barely. I don't think there's any going back now."

"Ghost?" Hammett twitched. "You don't think she's—"

"I don't know." I tried to get the upgrade to do something,

anything, that might be useful if things got ugly. I was sure they'd be getting ugly soon. "I've got a bad feeling about that space-walking corpse."

"You're not going to get yourself in any trouble, are you?" The pig's brown eyes watched me warily, and its nose scrunched up.

"That doesn't sound like me."

"'Straight forward cases,'" Hammett quoted at me. "'The pissant stuff the HCPD can't be bothered by but that might make a difference in some poor sap's life.' That's what you wanted to do."

"If I'm right about this, we're going to make a difference in a lot of lives. I just hope it's not going to make the big difference in mine."

"Why did you head for the beaches when you did?"

"Just testing a theory," I said. Then my tattler pinged and Weiland's ugly mug hovered in front of me. I blew a long breath out through my teeth and answered the call.

"Marlowe?" The wide orator's mouth was pulled down in a frown, and his grey eyes fixed on me. My 'gram would be tough to see on his end, hidden as I was in a dark room with only the dim pink light of Hammett's skin to illuminate me. Once he spotted me he let loose a barrage of words I hadn't heard used in earnest since grade school.

"Easy on the ear canals, Tommy Boy." I shook my head to

knock some of the really foul ones into my long term memory. "I'm having regrets about this call already."

"You'd better have regrets about more than that." A fat vein pulsed over his left eyebrow. "What's the big smoke, here? I told you to back off."

"I did back off," I said. "I backed right out of your jurisdiction."

"You said you were keeping your nose clean."

"I remember." I tapped the end of my nose with a metal finger. "You offered to rearrange it for me if I didn't."

"That's not what I—"

"Listen, Weiland. I don't want to have anything to do with you any more than you do with me. Your own limbs probably have expiration dates stamped on them just for being my ex-partner. So what do you gain by calling me up and haranguing me? I took this job based on false information provided by the client. I've tried to uphold my end of our deal. But I can only do so much looking the other way when I'm getting strung up for murders I didn't commit and dodging bullets from HCPD and tripping over headless corpses left, right, and centre."

"You've got the wrong idea, Bubs. I—" He blinked and rubbed at the vein with a thick, neatly manicured finger. "How many corpses are we talking about?"

"The left and the right at least." I folded my arms across my chest, suddenly remembering I was still in the deconstructed wet suit. "If we're only counting headless ones, but the centre is around here somewhere."

Weiland closed his eyes tightly and rubbed his face with his mitts like he was trying to erase some image behind his eyeballs. "You've got to get out of there. Swain's gunning for you with everything he's got. I mean on both sides of the law."

"Swain's going to have to cool his heels until I get back to Terra Firma unless he's got connections up here," I said.

"He's got more connections than sense," Weiland said. "And I can't get a hold of him to test the waters. I don't know what he's up to anymore. It's making me nervous."

"Well he's got some stiff competition to get to me first. Tell me, when's the last time you saw our friend Whip Tesla?"

"What happened the last time you started nosing around about that low-level grifter? Lay off, already."

"I've got him pegged for our benevolent beheader," I said. "I knew I recognized that gym-rat swagger, but his voice clinched it. I know it from our bust. What were you doing at techRose that night, anyway? Was Swain behind that set up?"

"LeRoy Lemieux called to complain about someone bothering his girls," he said. "I didn't know it was you. Your name didn't come up with Swain until after the fact."

"Isn't that convenient." I gave him a good sneer, one I'd been working on for a while. "You always work undercover for greasy club owners like LeRoy?"

"I wasn't undercover," he sighed. "I was off duty. A personal favour."

"Well he's dead now," I said. "You might as well spill the beans. LeRoy was in with Tesla, wasn't he? They didn't like me asking questions. Do you know why?"

Weiland ground his teeth the way he used to when I'd had too much to drink and he was trying not to say something I'd make him regret. Like then, he said nothing.

"Know who Tesla played for before Swain recruited him?" I pushed some more. "Chief is in way over his balding pate on this one."

"You'd better not be in bed with Punch Blanco, Bubbles."

"My bed is none of your business, Weiland. But it's sweet of you to care."

"Sweet, my hairy—" He undid the top button of his uniform grey shirt and ran a finger under his collar. "Just lie low and let me handle this, would you? I'm trying to help you."

"Is the loyal dog about to bite the hand of its master?" I leaned toward the 'gram and eyed the sweat on his forehead. "You're a wily son of a bichon, Weiland. But you'd be cuter with a bowtie. Are you up for promotion?"

"You are an infuriating woman."

"That's one of my better qualities," I said. "You really want to help me out? Go check in on Dickie Roh and make sure he's okay. If he is, give him a kiss on the teeth from me. It's one of his bright ideas that got me into this mess."

"I'll check on him." Detective Tom Weiland leaned back in his chair and sighed heavily. "If you'll promise me something."

"I can make promises," I said. "But at this point, I've made a few too many to keep them all."

"Don't get yourself killed, Bubbles." His big shoulders slumped and for the first time I noticed the bags under his deeply set eyes. "Swain isn't worth it."

"That much we can agree on," I said. "Swain's a mutated guppy in this cesspool, Weiland. And if my life's going to be worth more than a fart in the undercurrent, I have to square up with the big fish."

The corner of his mouth curled for a second before he remembered he didn't like me anymore. He cleared his throat. "Just don't get to thinking you're one of the sharks when you're only the bait."

I gave him a mock salute and killed the transmission. Hammett blinked its big cartoon eyes at me from the other side of the closet and shook its head. "Completely incomprehensible."

I wiped the stupid grin off my own face by letting it slide into a grimace. "I didn't lie to him."

"If either of you believes half of the things you say to one another, you're both lying to yourselves."

"Self deception. One of the many perks of being human." I jumped off the box and rummaged in my backpack for another set of clothes. "Where's the challenge in playing it straight?"

Hammett snorted. "You're both plenty challenged."

"I knew I should have put a limit on that adaptive personality upgrade." I pulled on a pair of shiny pink pants that had too many zippers and not enough pockets and unfolded my boots from the bottom of the bag. I opted to keep the bathing suit top and shrugged my old jacket, fuzzy side out, over it. "What kind of security do we have at Fortune's Favour?"

"Whyte didn't give us that kind of clearance." Hammett wiggled its curly tail.

I put my fists on my hips and narrowed my eyes at the pig. "But …"

It projected a holomap into the darkness with pale-blue dots marking guards patrolling the corridors outside the game rooms and stationed at each entrance. A silver dot glimmered at one of the tables. Other dots, black, milled around the various rooms and hallways, probably leaking a steady stream of cred behind them. I sent the map to my glasses and set Hammett back on the floor.

The pig said, "I think I'm getting better."

"Better." I gave one last look at the jumble of smooth metal limbs hanging from the walls of the bot storage closet and pursed my lips. "But the tail wiggle was a dead giveaway."

"Humph."

I experimented with the hydraulics in my new upgrade and got a feel for the range. Then I grinned. "Time to play with the new toy."

"It *sounds* like fun." Hammett squeezed its pink rump through the door and into the hallway. "But I guess you wouldn't have that look on your face if we were going to have a tea party."

I squeezed my own pink rump through and kicked the door closed behind me. "Now you're catching on. We might make you a P.I. Piggy after all."

"I suppose it's better than the hockmarket," Hammett grumbled. Then it led the way into the synthetic flotsam of the *Island Dreamer*, cesspool extension in the stars.

CHAPTER 14

The game rooms occupied their own half-level on the ship. It was the only area of the *Island Dreamer* that hadn't been painted with the same slick brush of comforting pastels and glossy neo-synthetics. The entire level had been done up like an ancient casino, as if the ideal environment in which to gamble had been discovered a thousand years ago and it obstinately refused to change again.

The floors were a writhing sea of black and gold and bright green with no place for the eye to land. Glowing signs and shiny machines covered in blinking lights plastered themselves to every available perpendicular surface. The ceiling was a labyrinth of grotesquely outsized chandeliers and mirrored tiles set at off-kilter angles so that the entire level felt like the inside of a broken kaleidoscope. Customers stumbled about in a razzle-dazzled daze of flying credits and assault by sensory stimulation, leaking cush from every hole in their bodies. Dinging and pinging and ringing, catchy little electronic tunes, and the relentless ka-ching-ing of tattlers' ceaseless one-way-only drain on holocred accounts flooded the ear canals. It oozed into the brain, sing-songing the mantra of gamblers throughout time and space across the entirety of the universe, 'One more time…'

A small balcony looked out from the gaming level, the only concession to sanity that I could find. Huge mirrored pillars hung from the ceiling here, breaking up the tranquil view of the rest of the ship with the reflected scenes of saturnalia, meant to both distract patrons from the outside world and to lure them back if they got too close to the edge. I stood there with the frenetic cush carousel spinning behind me, sucking in deep breaths as if I could compress and take the pastel calm with me like an oxygen tank for deep sea diving.

"You're going to hyperventilate if you keep breathing like that," Hammett said from between my feet. The pig stared into the chaos with wide eyed fascination, reflected lights gleaming in its cartoonish gaze. "I want to explore."

"You have to keep an eye on that silver dot," I said. "Tell me if she moves. If I try to read the map and navigate this zoo, my brain is going to explode."

"What about security?" Hammett spun in an impatient fig-ure eight over my boots and through my legs.

"What about them?"

The pig stopped. "These guys are staring at us."

"They're probably suspicious of all the money we're not spending."

Hammett flashed the map at me, and I turned back to the sprawling white canvas below so I could see it better. The security guards were lit up in blue. There seemed to be more of them than when we'd checked at the beach. "Do we want to avoid them?"

"For now, we're just going to find the girl. Whyte should have told his team to expect me. But if you notice any one of them paying too much attention—"

"Can we have a code word?" Hammett snapped to attention.

"Sure," I said. "If you see anything funny, just say 'I'd like a bacon sandwich.'"

The pig glared up at me. "I'm not sure that's appropriate for a—"

"We don't need a code word, Ham." I reached down to pat its little white capped head. "You have a direct line to my ear tubes."

"You never know. We could be monitored."

I gave a final, fleeting look at the lucidity of the real world and then laughed. Real world? Less than 48 hours ago, the *Island Dreamer* represented a high-cush world of luxury completely beyond my metallic grasp. Nothing on the ship was real. The only real thing I had was the promise of a slow and painful death if I didn't wrap this business up in a such a way that put me in the clear with Chief Swain and his army of criminal hopefuls. I shook my head and prepared for my dive into chaos. "Let's go. Before I decide to forget the whole thing and go back to my room and take a bubble bath in Lucky Bastard gin."

Hammett killed the map and trotted beside me, speaking into my cochlear implants. "It's not that bad, is it?"

"Everything about this place makes my skin crawl, Ham." I scanned the sweating, blank faces of the virtual lottery terminal zombies—what I could see of them beneath their headsets—feeling sick at the disjointed way their arms and hands floated in front of them, pulling and twisting and grabbing at knobs and leavers and credits that weren't really there. Out on the floor, similar wet-putty looks plastered the faces of people slumped around tables, laughing and chatting up their neighbours with as much heart as taxidermied sea-slugs. "At least down in the Grits we know we're a bunch of down-and-out zeros dragging our way through life on ragged fingernails. Up here, the highbinders are flying and credits are pinging. But it's the same sorry organisms peering out of those soul-dead eyes. They don't have it any better than we do. Worse maybe. They don't even know why they're unhappy."

Hammett pranced along in front of me with the curly pink tail of its pig skin bouncing along, and big eyes reflecting the dazzling lights. "I think it's great!"

"Enjoy it while it lasts. If I survive this trip, we're not leaving my apartment for at least a year."

Security didn't pay us any special attention once we had entered the fray. I didn't look cushy enough to be a mark or frazzled enough to pull something stupid, I guessed, so I blended into the background noise like a fuzzy pink shadow. I kept my opalescent glasses over my eyes to fit in with the other card sharks and made my way toward Game Room Twelve, Fortune's Favour, the sink hole dedicated to blackjack and poker and whatever variations on the theme were playing those days.

The main artery of the casino was a sprawling cathedral dedicated to cardinal sin. Luxury prizes spun on huge, glittering discs at strategic locations across the floor with half-naked hawkers flashing ticket machines and uptown accessories and exotic food and drink like their lives depended on it. Depending on who ran the admiral's casinos, maybe it did. Lorena Valentia had bought an entire holowall to advertise their copycat-chic "Stargazer" boutique line. Cosmo Cosmetics "Big Bang" didn't rate up here, surprise, infinite surprise. I turned left at a revolving display of a state-of-the-art gaming console complete with suspension tank and life support systems. It looked more like a space ship than the bangtails had. From there, I followed Hammett into one of the tubular corridors that sluiced off of the heart of corruption and deeper into the body of the beast.

As we approached Fortune's Favour, Hammett came to a sudden stop. Skin scanner cameras pointed down at the crowd but here, no one's outlandish outfits flickered or glitched for security. The high-stakes tables were skin-free zones, so players had to rely only on their carefully neutral faces or the distraction of their natural assets. There were a lot of natural assets on display. Hammett sat in the middle of the corridor with its pink ears drooping almost to the floor.

"Skin-banned again?"

The pig's little round head nodded morosely. Even its perky white cap seemed to sag beneath the glare of the cameras. "It's not fair."

"Tell you what," I said, keeping an eye on the door to Fortune's Favour. "Why don't you take the VLT vouchers that came with the Lucky Bastard prize package and play some slots for me. I'll check on the girl and be right back."

Hammett's ears flicked up so quickly one of them flipped inside out. It whipped its head around to look at me. "Do you mean it?"

"Sure," I said. "You aren't banned from the chance games as long as your winnings are deposited into a registered account. Go play your heart out. Just don't spend any actual money."

"Not even my winnings?" The pig deflated a bit.

"If you have any winnings, they stay in the account. I can't afford an AI with a gambling habit."

"Okay." Hammett nuzzled my shin. "You're not so bad, you know. I don't really mean most of the things I usually think about you. Thanks, Bubbles!"

"Hey!" I called after the little pink bottom hustling through the crowd. "What do you usually think about me?"

But the pig was long gone and, despite our comm link and my aural implants, was ignoring me completely. I muttered something churlish and hoped the traitor could hear me. Then I turned back to the problem at hand. The sooner I found the girl and verified my suspicions, the sooner I could get out of the glitter hole and back to my normal life, circling the drain in the Grit District gutter. I had just crossed the high-stakes boundary and was pointing myself in the direction of Game Room Twelve when a flash of iridescent sequins caught my eye. I turned my head just in time to see a now-familiar silver dress slip into the crowd in a different corridor. Cursing, I shoved my way past the horde of sweaty brows and glazed eyes clogging the corridor, and followed the girl.

She stayed just at the edge of my vision, flitting in and out of the crowd like a wraith. I pawed and clawed through the thickly packed bodies with my upgrade. The method earned me a few scowls, a couple of winks, and at least one angry tirade as I fought to keep up with my mark, but I had her by the tail. Somewhere behind me, a jackpot klaxon blared and the onslaught of bodies pushing toward the main floor seemed to swell with vicarious excitement and the anticipation of the next big win. Everyone rushed to see which game had paid out or which table had found the luck and headed toward the electronic beat throbbing from the centre.

"Free drinks!" someone hollered and the crush pressed on. For a ship full of cush-drunk wastrels, there was a whole lot of hubbub about diluted gratuity cocktails.

The woman's slim, brown leg disappeared around a corner up ahead and I pressed myself against the wall to slide past the suffocating mass of people swarming into the corridor from elsewhere in the casino. I was about to follow her out of the throng when something tightened around my neck. A woman had grabbed the back of my fuzzy pink hood and slapped at my face with long clawed fingernails.

I grabbed her wrists and shouted in her face. "What's the ruckus?"

The verbal excrement spilling out of her prettily painted lips made even my toes curl. She wore a dress like an upside-down cyclone of gauzy grey lace, loose and flowing at the bottom and wrapping in a tight spiral around her neck. The whole thing glittered with mirrored flecks of precious metals and gemstones. Above the getup, her eyes flashed a dangerous bloodshot red. Her unfocussed gaze swung wildly from me to the other people in the crowd. Beneath my fingers, her skin felt cold and clammy. Her pulse hummed in her wrists as she tried to twitch away from me, still screaming.

"Security!" I tried to flag a powder-blue uniform over the heads of the crowd. The girl stumbled and slipped off her platform shoes, falling forward into my arms. Frothy white saliva pooled inside her mouth and spilled out over her glitter-painted cheeks. Her eyes rolled back into her skull as if to check out what her brain was up to in there. Then her entire body convulsed, contorting her limbs toward her torso like the legs of a dead beetle. "Medic! We

170

need a medic!"

A small circle of space formed around us as the other passengers attempted to avoid getting involved. A few stuck around to watch. A woman in a pink robe stood at the back of the crowd. Between the shoulders of the people in front of her, a glimpse of her blank, smiling face gave me chills. There was something seriously wrong with those cultists.

I crouched next to the girl, alone, as she danced out the last of her life on the psychedelic carpet with an army of polished shoes and high-heels shuffling hastily past. The woman in the silver dress was long gone by the time a paramedic unit arrived. I watched numbly as a man in a red medic uniform tugged away the tall, geometric lace of her collar to take her vitals. I still held her wrists in my hands, as they announced her time of death. And when the paramedic took his hands away, I saw a clear teardrop shaped gem glinting against the pale white flesh of her throat.

CHAPTER 15

C lear? Or empty?

What was in the necklaces?

The Patti sim hadn't seemed to know about the others. But the dead girl's behaviour didn't rate for a tech-reaction to Tropical Punch. I backed away from the girl slowly, not wanting to draw attention to myself. But the paramedics were preoccupied with trying to haul the girl's body onto a maglev stretcher. When I got to the corner, I ran. The crowd was thinner here, and I was able to keep up a respectable pace for someone who sneered at exercise unless it was to chase the Kreme Kween doughnut cart down the street. The woman in silver had at least a ten-minute head start, though, and I had no idea what direction she'd be heading in this ship the size of a city.

"Hammett?" I tried to connect to gambling hog as I huffed down the corridor. "Where is she going, Ham?"

"This is so exciting!" a piggy voice squealed in my tubes.

"You're not the one running," I snapped. "Which way did she go?"

A pinging noise came through the earpiece and cheers broke out. "Sorry about that. Which way did who go?"

"The silver dot, you useless swine." My brain throbbed behind my eyeballs and all the patterns and blinking lights weren't helping. "I know she came down here, but I don't know where to turn next."

"She's still sitting at the table in Fortune's Favour." Hammett snorted. It sounded like a laugh. "I told you I'd keep an eye on her. Why are you breathing so hard?"

I stopped dead. "Say that again?"

"This is so much fun, Bubbles. You'll never believe what—"

"The silver dot is where?"

"Still at the table." Hammett snorted impatiently. "Now let me tell you what—"

"No time, Ham." I snapped. "Stay there. Keep and eye on the dot. Let me know if she moves."

"I am, but, Bubbles—"

"Meet me back at the room in one hour." I rolled my eyes and said, "I'd like a bacon sandwich. I'm going dark, Ham. Ping me if she moves."

I didn't wait for the response. I killed the default connection to the ship's navigation systems and turned off all comms except basic transmissions between me and the SmartPet. I ducked into a dark corner where some of the ship's stranger architecture overlapped into a cluster of broken lines and geometric vomit. It didn't go anywhere, but it made a nice little hidey-hole. I flipped another connection back on. The tattler made a sing-song chime in my ear tubes that wouldn't be heard by anyone else, and I waited for the other line to pick up.

A sketchy 'gram hovered in the air above the tattler in my upgrade. It was mostly blue static, but it looked like it was looking at me. I said, "Rae?"

"Bubbles?" The audio came through okay. "Where are you? Your connection is terrible."

"I had to drop off the ship's grid, Rae. I'm surprised we got any connection at all. I need your help."

"Are you okay? What's going on?"

"Please tell me this new rig you got me has plasma rockets or EMP grenades or something. I'm up against something big here. I need backup."

"I specifically chose that prototype because it doesn't have any firearms." Rae's voice kicked up a notch and the static buzzed angrily. "What is going on?"

"I can't tell you. I'm being monitored somehow, and I don't

know how much they can see or hear right now. I'm afraid to even think what I think I'm thinking. What can the arm do? Give me a rundown. Maybe I'll come up with something."

"Well …" Rae trailed off, suddenly much less confident than her usual badass self. Her face came into focus for a moment, and she blinked at me from behind her big-framed glasses. "It's a bit bourgeoisie, really. It was never intended for … whatever it is you do … I was mostly excited by its *potential*. I didn't know you were going to run off to outer space and get yourself into trouble with some international drug cartel."

"International *what*?" I said. "What in the name of sweet cush are you talking about?"

"It's all over the feedreels down here," Rae said. "Swain's out for blood. He's pegged you for being one of Punch Blanco's henchmen … henchwomen … people …"

"Forget Swain," I said. "He's got a bug up the wrong bung hole. I'll deal with him later. Right now, I need to know what I can do with this hunk of metal besides grab and punch."

"That's usually all you need!"

"There is nothing usual about this job, Rae. I'm in serious danger of taking the big sleep up here, along with everyone else on the ship, so make with the goods."

Rae sighed. "Well, you've got instant access to all the buzz networks, feed reels, socials, that kind of thing. It live vlogs to a preset channel, so you don't even have to have your own accounts—"

"I can't afford those kinds of connections! Am I going to get a bill for socials next month? I don't even know how to use that trashtech."

"Not while it's registered as a prototype," she said. "Libra's picking up the tab. But that's not all. There's a heartrate monitor, and a calorie tracker that logs consumption and expenditure automatically, a hydration monitor. You can scan food and beverages for a true nutritional profile and list of contaminants before you even put it in your body. It comes equipped with an entire array of guided meditation simulations that you can use with your visilenses. I'm getting a data-stream from you right now. You need to drink more water. Your blood pressure is a little on the high side …"

I rubbed my eyeballs and tried to push them back into my skull. "I'm about to have a rage stroke, Rae. Is that all it does?"

"What do you mean by all? It's got state-of-the-art biometrics. Celebrities use that kind of equipment to stay in shape. Since you quit drinking, I thought—"

"What, that I might want to start my own feedreel channel and vlog my personal journey to health and wellness? If I don't come up with a plan here, I'm going to be torn apart limb from limb and hand fed to Swain like Grit District sushi. How's that going to be for ratings, do you think? Please tell me there is something else on this thing. Some kind of weapon, please."

"Well, there's the grapefruit knife," she said. "Oh, um, your blood pressure is—"

"Okay, that's enough. Thank you for the lovely gift. If I somehow manage to survive this holiday, I'll take you out for meditation and grapefruit, and we can laugh about that time I almost died of not being bougie enough to understand my upgrade."

"I'm sorry, Bubbles. I thought—"

"I know. It's okay. I'll be fine. If you see Dickie, please tell him to stop giving my business cards out to drug dealers. It's not helping my rep with Swain."

The blue static fuzzed into focus long enough for me to see a well-arched eyebrow peeking above the thick frame of Rae's glasses. "You have business cards?"

"Goodbye, Rae," I said. "In case I don't make it out of here … Jimi didn't die in vain. He was trying to do the right thing for the wrong—"

A shadow crossed in front of the entrance to my hidey-hole and a powder-blue uniform blocked my exit to the corridor. I killed the transmission and blocked the comms again and pushed myself as far as I could into the dark recess. The man's back was to me and he had a hand up to his right ear as if he were receiving instructions. He planted his feet wide and looked like he planned to stay for a while. Great. I crouched low and peered between his legs, but I didn't see any other uniforms in the corridor.

I pounced on the man's back and wrapped my upgrade

around his throat, pulling him into the darkness with me. His legs thrashed and his fingers clawed uselessly at my arm, but he didn't make a sound. Once he was out, I pulled him the rest of the way into the recess and pulled out his communication implants. Lucky for me, the admiral hadn't sprung for the internal wiring. If I was right about the thing I was afraid to be thinking, it was probably lucky for the admiral too.

This guy had the clean-cut look of a legit *Island Dreamer* security goon, unlike the flakes that hit me on the holobeach strip. I considered relieving him of his uniform, but it was too big for me, and I'd stand out even worse as a phony blue boy than I did as a badly dressed socialite. So I checked his pulse to make sure I hadn't done any lasting damage, tucked him in carefully out of sight from anyone walking by, and slipped back into the corridor.

The silver dress was nowhere to be seen, of course, but I had an idea where to look. Not having access to the holomap made it nearly impossible to get there, though. I'd have to come up with another plan of attack. Taking a wild guess at the right direction, I turned another corner and found myself in a disorienting tunnel of swirling holographic colours. Rainbow vapours twisted round the edges of the tunnel like the outer lip of a whirlpool. Not many people traversed the kaleidoscopic path.

A young man with purple-black skin in a startlingly white leotard stood in the centre of the aisle, laughing as the colours swirled over this clothes and skin. The fabric might have been applied with a paint brush for all the coverage it offered, tucking into every nook and cranny like a Grit District pro skirt sucking up holocreds. A faint white stripe of hair split his otherwise clean shaven skull into two neat halves. A gauzy silver fabric connected his wrists to his shoulder blades, and trailed out behind him like the ephemeral wings of an intergalactic fairy.

"It tickles," he shouted. "Like little fish nibbling."

"Told you he was holding out the glow." Another three passengers, decidedly less glorious, shook their heads and made for the main casino. His friends, I supposed. A pale woman in a dull yellow blazer with nothing underneath but some sub-dermal piercings grazed me with her elbow as she passed then glared at me for getting in her way. She snapped her shaved head back and called, "Drift, you cosmic vetch, we're going to be late for the opening!"

The trio disappeared around the corner, leaving their friend spinning in the hololights. White eyeshadow swept all the way up to his eyebrows and an iridescent pink sheen glistened on his pouting lips. Strategically placed glitter highlighted his cheekbones that could have been made from cut glass. He was like an anthropomorphized galaxy dancing in the rainbow holotunnel. He ignored the trio as they disappeared around the corner and headed for the high-stakes rooms.

I advanced toward him cautiously in case he was on something more volatile than the usual euphorics, but he spun to face me with a sharp, lucid look in his obsidian eyes. He flicked his gaze over my body, left to right, up and down. Then he grinned with big, white teeth to match the rest of his outfit.

"Hush," he whispered to himself. "A vision approaches."

I cleared my throat, trying to remember how to talk to normal people. As if this guy was normal. "I like your lipstick."

"The confection speaks." He fluttered his eyelashes at me. "Thank you. I made it myself."

"Hey." I stepped a little closer. "I'm having trouble with my holomap. Can I—"

"The oldest play in the book." He reached out his gauzy winged arms and touched my cheeks with long, unpolished fingers. Colours danced over him like watery butterflies. "If you want my autograph, all you need to do is ask, poppet. For you, I'd do anything."

"Autograph?" I stepped back, scanning my brain for a memory of his face but the old flesh file came up with nothing. "No, I just need to get out of the casino. I'm looking for—"

"For a way out." He ran a finger along the inside edge of his plunging V of his neckline which dropped dangerously low. "Out of this place, and out of those clothes …"

"Never mind." I waved him away and made for the other end of the rainbow tunnel. "I'll find someone else."

"Sweet," his throaty whisper followed me. "A shy one. Don't worry, my little bon-bon, I'm offline. I always unplug when I'm on a vay-cay."

He grabbed hold of one of the pink fingers on my upgrade.

I grabbed back. I twisted his finger and yanked him toward me with a sharp jerk so that his arm bent behind his back and his glittering wings crumpled up between our bodies. "Who are you?"

"Okay, the hard-to-get act was cute." He whimpered. "Now you're just being mean."

"I'm serious." I twisted the finger a little harder. "I've had just about enough of surprises today. Who do you work for?"

"Ex-squeeze me?" He wound himself up into a tight little knot in order to glare at me with his immaculately painted eyes. "I've been a hustler my whole life, baby. From the grotty Grit strip to the Highbinder Haciendas, you know? Cosmo Régale works for no one but himself."

I let him go. "As in Cosmo Cosmetics?"

He rubbed the circulation back into his hand and narrowed his eyes at me. "You've got my brand smeared all over your ungrateful little mouth, and you didn't even recognize me?"

"Blood of my Enemies."

"A personal favourite of mine." He wrapped his fingers around a jutting pelvic bone and cocked his hip at me. "I *thought* you were a fan."

"I am, actually. I just didn't—"

"I know how it is. The fawning dwindles when the live feed dies." He turned away from me in disgust. "But I need time to myself, too, you know. I can't be on 24/7. There *is* still such a thing as privacy, isn't there?"

"Sure," I said. And, not knowing what else to say, I was honest. "I can't afford the vlog reels. I had to save up to buy a single tube of BoME."

Cosmo gave me a sidelong glance. "That pack of poseurs thought I wouldn't notice that they were wearing Valentia knock offs."

"Good riddance to cheap trash, then."

He crossed his arms in front of his body like he was warding off the plague, scorn dripping from his diaphanous wings like liquid silver. Then he waved them away and held his hands out in a cup for the holographic rainbow to pool inside. "You can feel it, can't you?"

I help out my fingers. The colours tingled across my skin faintly. I said, "It is like little fish."

"Good." He snapped his long fingers. "You pass. Come with me."

"Pass what?" I said. "Where are we going?"

"You want to get out of here." He sashayed out of the rainbow tunnel. "I'm done with this scene myself. As if I want to go to Valentia's opening after all that dizzy vetch has done to me. 'Stargazer' my immaculately waxed assets. I could use someone like you, you know."

"I've been hearing that a lot lately," I said.

He beckoned over his shoulder, and I followed. "Where do you want to go?"

"Back to my room." I fell into step beside him, having to hurry to keep up with his long, elegant strides. "I have to meet—"

"I'll take you there myself." He pursed his lips and raised an eyebrow at me. "If you ask me nicely I might stay a while."

"I don't think—"

"No, don't think. Nothing good ever comes of it." He stopped suddenly. "But first, I need you to do something for me."

"That depends on what you think I can do for you."

He caressed the smooth pink casing on my upgrade. His upper lip trembled. "Do you know how to use this thing?"

"It's not the vibrating model if that's what you mean."

"No." He licked his lips and sighed. "What I need is slightly more … primitive."

"It grabs, it climbs, it lifts heavy things. Makes big holes when I need it to." I made a fist. "The whole Pleistocene package."

"Perfect," he said. "Come with me."

"Where are we going, exactly?"

"We're going to make a big hole." He batted his eyelashes over his shoulder at me again. "And I don't mean the fun kind."

CHAPTER
16

"I never use holomaps." Cosmo tapped his temple with a carefully filed fingernail, so bare in comparison to the rest of his outfit that it evoked embarrassment to notice, like accidently walking in on your mother getting out of the tub. "Dulls the mind. No booze. No drugs. No feed access on weekends. I'm no Last Humanist, but creativity requires capital P Purity in order to stretch its wings and fly like a glittery space eagle, you know?"

I told him I knew, and followed him as he followed some kind of invisible sparkle trail out of the casino, through endless corridors, and into an elevator hidden behind another holoscreen. We went down.

"Those Valentia vetches couldn't even feel the rainbow.

That's the problem with pinches and drunks. Emotional extremophiles. There's no subtlety. Divine radiance has to burn so bright to get through the light of the glow-up or the dark of the burn out they only really comprehend sentiment by spackle knife. I mean, how is a Grit District gutter punk going to blow the cockwomble off the fashion industry when he's glowing so hot he thinks every back-alley peep show is the Erotic Ballet of Ganymede and Zeus? If you can't feel the rainbow, you can only reflect the bright lights and colours given off by the truly inspired, you know? Radiant as a dented chrome plate."

The inside of the elevator hummed in the silence that followed. Rounded, pearlescent walls, like the inside of a fish egg, absorbed the sound of his voice and held it, as if to spit it out at the first poor sap to step within its walls carrying a knockoff handbag.

"Yeah." I scratched my head. "Okay. I think I know what you mean. Where are we going again?"

The elevator made a pinging noise and Cosmo spread his iridescent space wings open with the door and flew out into a dazzlingly white corridor. Simple neon signs declared things like "Hangar 2B" and "Cargo III" along the right-hand walls. Various side passages branched off of the left like stray hairs left behind by a dull razor.

The self-proclaimed Gutter Queen of Cosmetics strode into the storage facility level like an artists approaching a blank canvas. "We are going to find my merchandise."

He swept past overhead hangar doors and code-locked jettison portals, inspecting each one and then abandoning it with a flourish of his thin black wrists. I hung back. "Your merchandise?"

"I don't know who she paid off." Cosmo stomped down the hallway like he was strutting the catwalk. "But I will find out. And I will use them as the before photo in my next Popup campaign."

"Valentia?"

"You think it's a coincidence that she booked the opening of her Stargazer lineup on the same luxury cruise as my Big Bang extravaganza? That third-rate skirt didn't even know about *Island Dreamer*'s maiden voyage until she found out I had it booked."

Who knew the cosmetics industry was as cut-throat as the drug syndicates? "If she's willing to sabotage you like that, what's to stop her from jettisoning your cargo at the corner of Tigris and Leonine?"

Cosmo put his hands on his hips and whipped around to face me with a visage like the enraged God of Stardust. "And miss out on the opportunity to scrape my pallets and rebrand my formula as her own? The woman is a snake, I tell you. The depths of her depravity are impossible to underestimate."

"You mean, over—"

"Shut up, Pinky. Bring your useful bits over here and help me blast this door into the next dimension."

"That sounds entirely unlawful."

"What are you talking about?" Cosmo bent at the hip so

that his mostly exposed chest was perfectly parallel to the floor, and inspected the seal behind the locker. "I can't steal my own merchandise. It shouldn't take much, I don't think. Just a little tap with that blushing beaut of yours and we'll be back in business. I will, anyway."

My eyebrows knotted together in such a twist I think I pulled a neuron. "You brought me all the way down here because you want me to vandalize a multi-billion-dollar space craft."

"Big Bang should be splattering the faces of every cush-drunk vetch on this space ship right now. Since when is it illegal to make dreams come true?"

"Uh … Do you want a list?"

"It's this one, right here. Just make a big hole in this general vicinity and I will prance in and rescue my razzle dazzles and la-dee-dahs. Then I'll take you to your room where we can—"

"This is the downside to sobriety." I ran my tongue over my teeth. "An intergalactic glitter fairy asks me to punch a hole in a rocket ship and here I am thinking about legal ramifications."

"Mmmhmm." Cosmo pursed his shimmering pink lips at me. "That's your problem right there. You're thinking again. True artists don't think. They react. I never think. My entire existences is a spontaneous reaction to the relentless stimulation of the universe, you know? I don't need drugs because I'm on a perma-glow from the inexorable potential of my own artistic expression."

"You're right," I said. "I do feel like punching something."

"You're offline. I'm offline. No one will ever know."

I crossed my arms over my chest. "You don't think an outfit like this has security cameras?"

"Nope." Cosmo swung his head back and forth like a seductive cobra. "The cameras are on the fritz. I ribbed up a few security guards to get the juice on Valencia because I *know* that lisping inferiority complex did it, but I can't *prove* anything, of course. They've got nothing in this section. It's all very hush-hush because who wants to admit a brand new cruiser like this one has electrical gremlins, you know? Maybe we're all going to die, but I am going to get my merch if it's the last thing I do."

"And you're sure it's this one?"

"Sure, I'm sure." Cosmo closed his eyes and massaged his temples, tapping his foot like the beat of a snare drum. "I was here when they loaded it. I remember."

I shrugged. It wasn't like I hadn't already punched through a door that day. The first was in the name of self-preservation. The second in the name of my favourite red-glitter lip product. It's not all that different when you're from the Grit.

I said, "To the Blood of my Enemies."

My upgrade hit the seam of the door just below the holoscreen keypad and my fist went straight through to the other side. I extended the piston in my wrist and pulled back with a kick from the hydraulics. The left side of the door tore off of its hinges and dangled there like a loose tooth.

Cosmo squealed and clapped his hands, then lifted a long, iridescent-white leg through the mangled opening and pushed his way into the cargo bay beyond. Somewhere inside the bay a high-pitched whining sounded out like the keening wail of a D-list lounge singer. A flawless plan. I was proud to be a part of it.

"Son of a motherless goat," he muttered. One of the diaphanous glitter wings snagged on a bit of twisted metal and tore in two.

"Move it." I unhooked his wing and pushed him the rest of the way through so I could follow him inside. "Let's get your goods and get out of here before the boys in blue show up. I'm already on the naughty list."

Cosmo's white lidded eyes widened, and he stared at me with eyes like black holes. His lips trembled. "You're a criminal?"

"Well, I am now." I shoved him forward. "Get your stuff. Let's go. It smells like a black-market dumpster in here."

The long-limbed glitter fairy took a few more steps inside and stopped dead. The pearly second skin on his right buttock twitched.

"Nope!" He spun on his heels with his hands over his eyes and stalked blindly back to the door. "Wrong one. This isn't my bay. I didn't see anything, though. Let's go."

Cosmo clawed his way past me, looking grey beneath his face paint, and shoved himself back through the hole to the hallway outside. I stumbled out of his way. "What are you—?"

The smell hit me first, like cheap jewellery held in sweaty palms. I crept forward slowly. The whining noise pierced my eardrums and reverberated off the walls and the towers of boxes that filled the cargo bay. Crates stacked up against every wall in the bay like silver building bricks. One tower leaned precariously, and another had toppled, as if it had been upset during a struggle. A crate with an open lid spilled its glittering contents across the floor. Hundreds of choker-style necklaces with drop pendants littered the ground at my feet. A few had landed, not on the sterilely clean corrugated metal flooring, but in a thick pool of viscous black-cherry liquid that had been smeared across the floor as if by a mop-wielding maniac. Bright red splatters painted the walls and the door to the airlock. A high-pitched hissing sound escaped from the door where it was attempting to seal around a lump of mangled flesh and hair.

I stumbled backward, and crunched a necklace beneath the heal of my boot. A thin pink fluid oozed out between the crystalline shards of glass. "Let's get out of here before that alarm brings half the fleet security down here. I need to find the Chief of Security."

I climbed through the hole after Cosmo. He stood there, snivelling and trembling with his hands shaking at the ceiling. "It wasn't us, officer. We just found her. We just—"

"Get the cuffs on him." The tall blonde security guard snapped. She had the same smushed face, and the same quick eyes. But she looked meaner now. Madder.

"So, uh… I know we got off on the wrong foot before," I said. "But we both work for Whyte. Right? Let's not do anything too crazy. We need to call this in to the admiral, immediately."

"What a coincidence." She held a small, deadly looking pistol in her right hand and motioned to the others with her left, pointing at me. "It was the admiral who sent us down here to pick you up. Looks like you bet on the wrong horse."

"I always put my money on the lame ones," I said. "Nothing like the threat of the glue factory to put a little pep in your step."

"And tase the pink one." The blonde gestured with her pistol. I flinched. "She's looks like she's about to resist arrest."

The skinny little rat-faced man stepped forward and grinned at me with his crooked yellow teeth. He held something small and black in his right hand. This time, I was the one without backup.

"I'm not—" The words died in my throat as a pulse of nerve-exploding pain shot through my body and I dropped, twitching, to the floor. Neither I, nor Cosmo, nor the powder-blue uniforms ever learned what it was I had been about to deny. And by the time I regained consciousness, I didn't remember what it was I had wanted to say in the first place.

CHAPTER 17

I came to in a cold, white cell. I rolled over and glared between my eyelashes at a smear of painfully bright lights, groaned, and sat up. My balance felt off. A low shelf, moulded out of and extending from one of the walls, became both a bed and a sitting area. I planted my bare feet on the white floor. My head throbbed. Cold oozed up the soles of my feet and into my legs. A hole in the corner with a grab bar made the toilet. A semi-transparent privacy screen was afforded in the toilet area, but it only provided enough coverage to add a little titillation for the unseen observed. I vowed not to use the thing if I didn't have to.

I wore a loose jumpsuit in a shocking shade of something that might have been orange or green and managed to land some-where in the vicinity of "upset stomach." My left shoulder ached.

I tried to move my arm but it wasn't there. The puke-coloured prison uniform had been neatly pinned up over my stump. The nerves felt raw, like whoever had removed the upgrade had done so with more fervour than finesse. I lifted my right hand and felt around my ears. The visilens glasses and the tubes were gone. At least they'd left me the plate that held my guts in. That would have been a mess.

I stood up carefully. My head did a poor imitation of a waltz before it had spun itself in enough circles to settle down and sit the next dance out. I closed my eyes. I opened them again. I tested a step or two and decided I probably wasn't under the influence of whatever sedative they'd hit me with after they'd tased me. One wall of the cell appeared to be made of mirrored glass. There I was. My bubble-gum-pink hair clashed horrendously with the prison jumpsuit, which was probably why they'd picked that colour. Vomit looks pretty bad on everything. At least my lipstick had stayed in place. Cosmo would be proud, wherever he was.

My stomach clenched at the empty space below my left shoulder. I had never gotten used to the fact that I was missing the arm. Rae had had me patched up with a cybernetic enhancement before I even knew I'd survived the blast that had been meant to kill me. The image in the mirror was an unfinished sketch of the way I saw myself in my head. All smudges and broken lines and identifying features rubbed out with a dirty eraser. I approached the reflection, studied this new incarnation. My nerves pulsed and twitched as I flexed fingers that weren't there. If I'd had my upgrade, I'd have punched a hole in something. My hair was a mess, the outfit was a travesty, but my eyes were clear and sharp. I took a deep breath. This was a class pile, but it could be worse. I put my flesh hand against the glass and pushed.

A door slammed open, so close to me that it almost took my elbow with it. Whyte stalked into the room with his pepperoni face peeking out the top of the dark-blue uniform. He didn't look so funny to me now. The sadistic little rat-faced guard stuck to Whyte's heels, shorter and even skinnier, like a diluted shadow. He held a plasma taser pointed carefully at my chest and twitched his raw, pink nose.

"You were supposed to watch her." Whyte's face contorted into a grotesque caricature of human features like rage had been carved into a hunk of old leather.

"At 1900." I said. "I checked on her at the beach and then hit the admiral's detail."

I glanced at the security guard behind Whyte, unsure how much he was supposed to know about any of this. Then I realized it wasn't my problem anymore. I'd be sent back down to the surface and handed to Swain on a silver platter at this rate.

"Did you kill her?"

That brought me up short. "Me? Are you kidding?"

"The cameras have been down since we left Terra Firma. I checked up on your so-called spacewalker and couldn't find a damned thing. Then I send a team in to do a physical sweep and what do we find? You and some poncey little man, returning to the scene of the crime. Thought you could go back and clean up before we got there, did you? See how far that got you?"

"Now, wait a minute," I said. "That doesn't make any sense. I'm the one who told you to go check down there. Why would I do that before I had cleaned up? Besides, Blondie said the admiral—"

"You're good." A malicious smile stretched across the Chief of Security's face, and there was no joy in it. Only a twisted kind of anticipatory pleasure. "You almost had me. You thought you could make a quick buck on me, eh? As soon as I asked you to check up on my wife, I saw the gears turning behind those gutter-punk eyes of yours. I know how people like you operate. The admiral was a fool to trust you on the word of a ..."

"Sir," the little man behind him sneered. "You want me to hit her again?"

"Not yet," Whyte cracked his knuckles and stepped toward me. "I want to hear it from her own mouth. You thought you'd follow her, maybe put a little pressure on, make some fast cash. But she wasn't putting up with it, was she? She wouldn't. I know her. Things got ugly and you lost your cool. It happens all the time, eh? Little better than animals down in the Grits. Isn't that right? But I'll tell you this. It doesn't happen on my ship. You're going to tell me what happened, and I'm going to make sure it never happens again."

I backed away from him with my hands up. One hand and a stump of fabric, anyway. "Did you look at her body yourself?"

"There is no body!"

"What's left of it, I mean," I said, keeping my voice calm. It was like talking down a raging pincher on the glow-down. "Did you see her face?"

"I'll say my goodbyes after the coroner has—" His voice cracked. "Goddamn you, Marlowe. How could you?"

"I'm sorry, Hank." I flinched as I said it, anticipating a blow. But it never came. The hard line of Whyte's navy-blue shoulders sagged and his face crumpled. "Your wife is dead. But it's not her in the cargo bay."

His eyes snapped to my face. "What?"

"I can't prove it yet, but I think she's been dead for a couple of days now," I said. "And she was missing for weeks before that."

Whyte's face twisted in another knot and he clenched his fists. "I just spoke to her this morning."

"Spoke to her, sure," I said. "But when's the last time you touched her?"

A long breath seeped out of Whyte's mouth and his shoulders sagged even farther, like he was deflating. "I should snap your neck. Who would care?"

"Listen to me, Hank. Your wife wasn't who you thought she was. You suspected as much yourself when you came to me. Well, it's true. But not in the way you thought. You promised me you wouldn't go crazy if I told you the truth."

"I promised you I wouldn't hurt *her*."

"If you kill me now, you will be hurting her." My eyes flicked

197

around the room, searching for a way out. Searching for anything that might help me. "You'll be hurting the cause she was fighting for. She was trying to protect—"

He lunged for me and grabbed the front of my prison suit in a red, leathery fist. He was a thin man, but I could feel his body wired with muscle beneath the blue uniform. "Be very careful what you say next."

Without my upgrade I was at a significant disadvantage against him. Even if you didn't count the fact that I was being held a gunpoint, in the prison cell of a spaceship flying through outer space. There was no escape. I figured I might as well try for the truth.

"Your wife helped to develop a nootropic drug for the Last Humanists," I said. "But the formula was highjacked by some low-level drug dealer from the Grit. She tried to stop the delivery but it all went sideways. Did you know she worked for the anti-techers? It's all connected. Her strange behaviour, the Last Humanists, the necklaces, the woman in the silver dress. I don't know how yet. But it is." I was babbling. Whyte's grip twisted, and he lifted me onto my toes. A big smoked-meat fist hovered over my face. "Wait! the only thing I know for sure is that it was your wife's body I found upstairs in techRose."

"What?"

"That's what started this whole thing. She wanted to meet me. Said she wanted me to deliver a message, but the message was just to make sure it was really me who came. She wanted to give me something."

A nervous voice, as pale and trembling as the man himself, piped up behind Whyte's shoulder. "You want me to shoot her?"

"No," Whyte said. Then his fist crashed toward my face.

Like a piston, he pulled it at the last second. Maybe he didn't really have the heart to mash my nose into mince meat. I had the good sense to grunt and fall down anyway. I buckled at the knees, and Whyte let go of my jumper. My body collapsed in a heap on the cell floor. I kept my eyes closed and let my head loll to the side so I could keep an eye on Whyte and his shadow through a cracked lid.

"You really nailed her, sir." The pink-faced man stared at my body and licked his lips. His hands shook. I hoped I wasn't going to get tased again. "What do you want me to do?"

"Watch her, McSweeny." Whyte snapped and the little man flinched. "I'm going to set up the interrogation room."

A thin smile spread across the man's pink face as Whyte stalked out of the cell. Men like that are the ones to look out for, not the big, macho, meat-fisted thugs or the guys in fancy suits with cush oozing out of every pore. They're bad enough, but it's those little guys. The ones that get stepped on by the big guys once too often and are itching to grind their heels into someone or something smaller than themselves. McSweeny had the look of a rosy-cheeked child about to pull the legs of a spider. He licked his lips again. "Yes, sir."

I felt McSweeny approach cautiously, like a rat investigating a trap. The sole of his boot brushed my right hand and hovered there. If I moved, I was going to get tased again. If I didn't move, bug boy was going to try to throw his weight around. First stop, my fingers. It started as a slow pressure. I held still and breathed deeply, preparing myself for what would come next. The joints popped as they crunched between the hard floor of the cell and McSweeny's foot. Talk about being stuck between the pin and the pincher. Pain exploded like a burning jolt of electricity from my hand and up my arm. I stayed still, letting the sensation flow through me as if I could make it stop by letting it pass over unacknowledged. I figured I'd wait until they moved me to try any funny business. But without my arm, it wasn't apt to be too hysterical on my end.

In any case, I didn't get the chance. Whyte came back and McSweeny pulled his foot away before he had a chance to break anything. Whyte brought in a stretcher and a cart just like the shopping scooters I'd seen down on the strip, chock full of all things sharp and pointy for all your flesh-rending, skin- tearing needs. Must have been a sale at the Torturers Tavern. They strapped me onto the stretcher, probably the same one they planned to haul me out on when they were finished, and all I could come up with was to play dead. My heart beat a little too hard in my chest for someone who was out cold, but they were too excited to notice.

From one of the other cells, I heard a man's voice pitched high with outraged screaming. "I'm telling you, it's Valentia! She sabotaged my show, she stole my merchandise, and she did that nasty business in the cargo bay. Don't you be fooled by her face. Her face is all right. But she could use a bag on that personality. Ugly, you know? Wrap a big 'ol burlap sack round it, tie it up with chains, and drop it on the bottom of the ocean. She's evil, you know? You know!"

There was a crash from somewhere, and a yelp. Then silence, except for the ragged, panting breath of the pink-faced lunatic. McSweeny's watery eyes had a bead on me. The lights shifted as the stretcher swung out of the cell and into the corridor between Whyte and his diluted shadow. My body slid noiselessly beneath the glaring overhead lights. Careful not to blink or twitch in case the gun-happy pappy in the powder-blue suit had set his taser to deep-fry, I counted my breaths and tried to slow my heart rate.

Whyte pulled the stretcher along with one hand and the cart along beside him. If it had been any proper kind of horror flick, the squeaking of rusted wheels would have cranked ominously along with us. Frankly, I felt a bit betrayed by the lack of attention to atmosphere. What kind of way was this to die? Framed for the death of the same woman, twice, and I hadn't even done it once. This was worse than my failure to die in Swain's training accident. If I survived, I vowed to commit some legitimate crimes. That way, the next time I got hammered by a sucker punch, at least I could die feeling like I deserved it.

A door shushed open somewhere in the vicinity of my head, and Whyte pulled the gurney into a darkened room. McSweeny slipped inside after him and flicked on the overhead lights. Whyte flicked them off again. He said, "Get her in the chair."

McSweeny twitched and put his taser on the cart full of torture implements. He wrenched on the straps of the gurney and I rolled over and groaned, but Whyte glared at me with such venom that I decided it was in my best interest to die quietly. The pink-faced minion dragged me off the stretcher and grunted beneath my weight. I had to be at least twenty pounds his superior, and I let him have it. It was all I had to give.

Eventually, he got me into a hard metal chair and belted me into some new restraints around my shins, my lap, and my chest. Blood dripped from my nose and into my mouth. I tried to wipe at it, but McSweeny yanked my only arm back down and pinched it into place with a rubberized belt. I was really starting to dislike the guy. When I was good and immobilized, I opened my eyes the rest of the way and looked hard at the Chief of Security.

"Please, Whyte," I said. McSweeny stepped in front me and sneered with a face like a naked mole-rat's ass. I leaned to the side to look at Hank. "Whatever you do to me, do it yourself. Don't give this little pissant the—"

I didn't get a chance to finish my final request. Whyte grabbed a syringe the size of a dagger off the cart and I flinched back, even though I knew there was no where I could go. Then he stabbed the needle into the mole-rat man's neck and hit the plunger. McSweeny's watery eyes rolled backward as if looking for his brain, and finding nothing, he crumpled to the floor of the cell.

Whyte tossed the empty syringe into the corner of the cell where it made a pretty little tinkling noise as it smashed on to the floor. He stepped over the powder-blue uniform and reached for me with his oven-roasted hands. His white teeth flashed as he said, "Now it's your turn, Marlowe."

CHAPTER 18

"It's safe to talk in here." Whyte dropped the act like a mask and smiled apologetically. He undid the straps that cinched me to the chair. "This interrogation room has never had any surveillance systems installed. They aren't just off. They can't be hacked because they don't exist. It's probably the only place on the ship that is truly safe to speak in right now."

"An off-grid interrogation room." I walked around the small room and inspected the walls, the ceiling, the corners, the lights. Under the chair. Not that I didn't trust him. I believed he believed what he was saying. "I can see how that might come in handy on a military craft. What the hell are you doing with one on a luxury cruiser?"

"You'd be surprised at the kind of people who decide to

take luxury cruises through international space when life on the surface gets a little too hot for comfort." Whyte pulled off the last of the straps and then opened a door at the bottom of the cart. My clothes and backpack were inside, along with my upgrade. "The admiral monitors them. If the right people make the right kind of offer, sometimes we cooperate with Trade Zone authorities."

"Since when is Punch Blanco an 'authority'?"

Whyte sighed and lifted my upgrade off the cart. He held it out to me, but I didn't take it. He said, "How did you know?"

"Just throwing darts in the dark," I said. "At this point, I'd have to be trying not to hit something funny. The admiral wanted me brought in. Why'd he roll on me?"

"The admiral is a powerful man, and he likes to keep it that way," Whyte said. "I'm not privy to the details, but I'd say he found the answer to his question on his own or someone offered him a better deal."

"I need your help with that." I gestured to the arm with my chin and started to undo the top of the hideous jumper. It took me a while with only one hand. I never had gotten very good at it. I shrugged my left shoulder out from under the fabric and appreciated the way Whyte didn't stare at the disfigured skin underneath. He could have gotten his eyeful when I was unconscious, I supposed, if he had wanted to. But he didn't strike me as that kind of guy. He slipped the socket of the upgrade onto my arm and held it while the connection plates synched up.

"The admiral received a call from Blanco a couple weeks

ago," Whyte said. "Telling him about the woman in the silver dress, and to watch out for her. Sent us a 'gram and when to expect her. She's been on the ship since not long after the call."

"Around the time that your wife began acting strangely." I went through a few of the standard nerve tests to make sure the arm's basic functions were intact. It wouldn't have the same finesse as if Rae had installed it, but it should do the trick until I got back to Terra Firma.

"She'd gone to the surface to meet with one of her colleagues," Whyte said. He stepped back while I put the arm through some wide, swinging arcs. "When she came back, she was the same, but different somehow. Distant. At first I thought she was having an affair."

"She didn't let you touch her after that."

"No," he said. "She even slept in a different room from me. I didn't put up a fuss. Like I said, I expected something like this to happen. But it killed me a bit too. Part of me always hoped that I was wrong, and that she really did love me. One night I peered into the room, just to look at her. Just to see her without that cold, distant look she had adopted."

"And that's when you began to suspect—"

"It was horrible." Whyte sat down in the interrogation chair and put his face in his hands. "She slept like she was a part of the furniture, completely still. Her eyes open at the ceiling. Her chest didn't move. I thought she was dead. I thought—" Whyte took a deep, shuddering breath. "But when I stepped into the room, she sat up fluidly and locked eyes with me and spoke in her cold voice, and I knew it wasn't her at all. She said, 'Leave now.' And I did."

"What's her connection to Blanco?"

Whyte put his hands on his knees and hung his head. "I don't know. I can't make any sense of it. She has never used drugs. She believed in that Absolute Purity bull with every cell in her body. I would have bet my life she didn't have any connections to the HoloCity underworld."

Her connection went deeper than that. If I was right, her connection to the Last Humanists was more sinister than any drug lord king pin could ever be. But I didn't think it would help to tell him at this point. "Did you know she was a Last Humanist when you married her?"

"Yes," he said. "I mean, she's doesn't wear the robes or anything. But she's an Absolutist. That was one of the things I liked best about her. She was so brilliant and beautiful and nothing about her was artificially enhanced or simulated."

"Aside from the lies."

Whyte winced slightly. "Right."

"And what about you?" I asked. "Are you Pure?"

Whyte rolled his shoulders and blushed. "That's not really any of your—"

"It could be important, Hank."

"I had them removed before Patti and I started dating." He

avoided my eyes. "I thought it would impress her."

"Very romantic," I said. "That little valentine might just have saved your sunburned butt. Now tell me, when we spoke in your office, you wanted me to go check on her at the beaches. Why?"

"I put a tracking dot on her favourite broach, one she wore almost all the time even after she changed. She kept hanging around the Amity Beach simulation, but she never went inside. I've tried to meet her there, myself, but—"

"She falls off the grid."

"I thought she was tracking me, too, that something alerted her to my presence like it had in our bedroom. I thought maybe you could find her when she didn't want to be found."

"I found her," I said. "As a simulation inside the Amity Beach holodeck."

Whyte's ice-blue eyes met mine forcefully. "And?"

"I spoke to her," I said. "She left a message for me. And something more than the message. A clue, hidden in her words."

I thought about the simulated necklace she'd dropped in my hand. The jolt of electricity. I didn't say anything about that. I said, "She was careful, though. She must have been scared."

"How do you know?"

"Just a hunch." I wasn't ready to lay all my cards down just yet. "But for one thing, there's a skin lock on the door. I think your wife got herself tangled up in the politics of her religion and couldn't get out again. Someone knows that you asked me to look into it, and that someone tried to follow me into the simulation."

"That's not possible." Whyte's voice came out in a scratchy whisper.

"How is a fly like the universe, Whyte?"

He stared blankly at me.

"Sometimes they are not exactly what they seem."

"My office?"

"You need to do a manual sweep. Get rid of any bugs, balls of lint, chewed up wads of gum stuck under your desk. It could be anywhere. Don't trust any scanners."

Whyte blinked at me. "That's impossible. We have—"

"The best security money can buy," I said. "Yes. We've had this conversation before. And yet this little fly slipped past your skin-screeners and has been feeding all your off-grid conversations into the ears of someone much bigger and meaner than you."

Whyte put his face in his hands and groaned. "The admiral is going to have a fit."

"The admiral is the least of our worries right now."

"Speak for yourself. I'll lose my job over this. And I already—" Whyte's shoulders heaved once, then shook. He looked up at me with tears in his hard blue eyes. He took a shuddering breath, closed his eyes, and said, "You really think she's dead?"

"I'm sorry, Hank."

"I wish it had been an affair."

"You really loved her." I crouched down next to him and put my flesh hand on his back. "I'll find out what happened to her. I wish I could do more."

"Tell me what you know."

I sighed and stood, rolling my shoulders as I paced the room. "I know a lot of bits and pieces, but I don't know exactly how they fit, yet."

"Try me," he said. "We don't have a lot of time. You need to get into McSweeny's uniform and out the door before anyone realizes you're gone. I caught this little rat phoning in your arrest to Swain."

I cursed under my breath. "I had almost forgotten about that idiot."

"He wasn't there," Whyte said. "Which means someone already gave him an idea. Depending on which bangtail he tried to catch, he could be—"

"I thought he didn't have jurisdiction up here."

"He doesn't. But the admiral does."

I cursed under my breath. "Swain doesn't need to arrest me to make my life hell. He's in bed with the HoloCity drug syndicates. Would the admiral let him board?"

"If he sees an opportunity he might cooperate, even with the likes of Swain, at least as long as it suits him."

"And if he's taking tips from Punch Blanco, who knows who else could be pulling strings."

"I don't know what's going on anymore."

I rummaged through the pockets of my jacket on the trolley and found a piece of gum. I chewed it slowly, thinking about how to answer him. "My suspicion is this: your wife hired me to find the girl in the silver dress. But Patti really wanted me to find her. She gave me a message to deliver, like a code, I think, to prove it was really me. She planned to meet me at techRose with some sensitive information. She'd been hiding out there for at least a week, maybe more, before she made the call."

"Why would she call you?" he said. "Why wouldn't she ask me for help?"

"She got my name from a friend of mine. They worked together. He has also, incidentally, gotten himself faded. I don't think she planned to call me, but my assistant flooded the Grit with business cards like the one you found. Patti must have found one, and kept it hidden, knowing she might have trouble."

"She was a scientist at Libra." Whyte leaned back in the chair and rolled his head back to stare at the ceiling. "They deal in cosmetic stuff. Upgrades, fashion skins, designer party drugs. It's not like she was working on some top-secret military intelligence. It doesn't add up."

"It does if your math allows for imaginary morals and the corruption of every function. We're talking about HoloCity." I ran my fingers through my hair and tugged. "Anything can be weaponized by the right kind of psycho."

Whyte crossed his arms over his chest and stared me down.

"This has nothing to do with my wife."

"Patti worked at Libra." I counted out the points on my fingers. "But she was undercover for the Last Humanist Church. They were developing a nootropic, a mental-performance-enhancing drug, designed specifically for the technophobes in the pink robes."

"Totally harmless," Whyte said. "Nootropics are a dime a dozen. They give them to kids in schools to increase their test scores."

"This one is different," I said. "By all accounts, it's much more powerful than anything on the market right now. And this particular formula triggers an immune response in the body of anyone with tech implants, causing the body to attack itself. My friend Jimi discovered this flaw and fixed the formula. And got himself killed for it."

"It doesn't make any sense."

"It's starting to. Listen to me. Your wife knew about the flaw in the formula and tried to stop it from being delivered to the leader. The Rose. She failed. I was there at the bust, but I didn't know *she* was until today. Swain tried to hush it up. Suddenly, Tropical Punch hits the market. It's either really good or really deadly, depending on the punch. I *knew* it was connected to our bust. I couldn't let it go. After Jimi died of an apparent drug overdose, I was rabid about it. Boom." I knocked my metal and flesh fists together and made an explosion. "Early retirement."

"So you think Swain leaked the flawed formula to one of his

drug king pins?"

"Trouble is, those syndicate guys love their upgrades." I remembered I was supposed to be getting out of here and began to shrug my way of the prison jumper, grateful for the full coverage undergarments that came with it. Then I started pulling on my own clothes.

"Wait," Whyte said. He bent over McSweeny and started unbuttoning the powder-blue uniform. "You'll need this."

I let him deal with McSweeny and continued to think out loud. "It looks like someone is targeting the syndicate because so many of these low-level drug barons can't help but sample their own merchandise. Swain's starting to smell a little less fresh at the top of the rat pile."

"You figure he wants the new formula." Whyte tugged off McSweeny's pants and hands them over to me. I pull them over my own pink pair and cringe. Blue has never been my colour.

"There are two ways this can play out," I said. "The only people to know about this new formula are dead. Someone wants it, or wants it kept secret."

"No one would want a drug that can only be used by Absolutists."

"No one except the Rose."

"But if the flaw was fixed—"

"Suddenly we've got a winner." I snapped my fingers. "Everyone wants it. And who is sitting pretty at the top of the

HoloCity drug market, doling out passes for who can deal what where?"

Whyte rubbed a weathered brown hand over his upper lip. "Swain."

"Patti was killed by a man named Whip Tesla," I said. "He worked for the Last Humanists too. The delivery boy Patti tried to stop. But when we busted the drop, he rolled over for Swain without so much as a doggy biscuit. I did a little dance with him at techRose after I found—"

Whyte's tanned leather skin was looking a little green.

"Sorry. The point is, Swain's man knew about my meeting with Patti. He killed her and another dancer, and probably Jimi too. But I never got whatever it was she wanted to give me. Which means Tesla got it. Which means Swain has it now. And I'm next on his snuff list."

"What are you going to do?"

"I need to get to the Rose," I said. "He's on the ship, isn't he? I want the truth this time."

"Shortly after Patti got back from HoloCity, we got a call from the admiral that we were being blessed by the presence of the Rose—the Last Humanist's leader—for *Island Dreamer*'s inaugural voyage. The admiral is always playing the political game, so it didn't strike me as that strange. Patti was thrilled about it. It's the most emotion I saw from her since..." Whyte yanked on the jacket and McSweeny's body rolled onto its face. He balled the jacket in his fists. "It wasn't her, though. I keep forgetting. After we got word about the Rose, Patti started ordering all these necklaces for the Platinum Package guests. Why would she do that?"

"Decoys," I said. Some of them, at least, but I didn't want to confuse matters anymore than they already were. "Just like the other women in silver dresses. It's a set up for Swain. They want him to think there's more than one batch of the formula. That's what I've been thinking. It didn't make sense when I thought it was me being jerked around on the short chain. But it's not me. I'm just here to sweeten the deal. I'm the pink icing on the bait cake."

"The admiral wouldn't let Swain board the ship unless …"

"Unless it became politically efficient, right?" I said. "Looks like it did. It wouldn't surprise me if Swain's got more cohorts than this little turd in the gene pool."

I gave McSweeny a nudge with the toe of my boot.

Whyte's face reddened. "I don't like it, but you're right. My authority is strangled unless I can get the admiral back onside."

"Swain's got at least one of his goons up here already, not counting sympathizers on your own roster. That mess in cargo has to be Tesla's work. My bet is the Rose has encouraged the admiral to let Swain make a personal arrest. That way they get the competition up here where there's a little more legal wiggle room, and they can deal with him as they see fit. The admiral didn't get too sentimental about our contract when he sent that team down to cargo for me. I'm at the bottom of the heap here. The only reason I had any real value was that Swain wanted me and the Last Humanists want Swain."

Whyte rubbed his temples. "If Swain took the bait and is on his way, we don't have much time."

"Where are the Last Humanists staying?"

"The official party arrived ahead of schedule," Whyte said. "We weren't expecting them until—"

I jabbed him in the chest with my finger when the realization hit me. "Tomorrow at 1900."

"Yes."

"You knew." I tucked my hair under the little white hat, feeling foolish. "You knew all of this was connected from the beginning, and you just let me ramble along, getting myself beat up and arrested."

"They arrived about the same time the patrol found you and Régale in the docks." Whyte put my backpack inside a security briefcase. "If I hadn't been preoccupied with the envoy, I probably could have delayed your arrest. I'm sorry about that. And I'm sorry I didn't tell you about the Last Humanists. I had suspicions, but nothing like this."

"Send me a map I can use off grid," I said. "I know what I have to do."

Whyte crossed his arms. "Why don't we just let the Rose take out Swain? You could stay here until I get things sorted with the admiral."

"And maybe you lose your job, and I get handed over to Swain before the cultists make their move." I shook my head. "Besides, who's to say I want the Rose to get what he wants? The Last Humanists don't exactly look highly upon the likes of people like me."

Whyte's expression flickered suddenly. He touched his throat. Something glinted under his collar. He looked at me with such a cold determination in his eyes I stepped back, my heart pounding. "You're right. Patti protected the Mezzanine Rose and their secrets. And they let her die like an animal."

"I'm sorry, Hank." I tried not to look at the thing around his neck. "Even the Purest humans aren't immune to greed and corruption."

He tried to pass me McSweeny's side arm. I waved it away. "No thanks. I've had my fill of things that go boom."

"When I open this door," he said, "keep your head down and go straight for the exit. Take the first lift to the passenger quarters. I'll get you your map."

"Watch your back, Whyte," I said. "Helping me might end up being a very expensive mistake."

"You help me bring Patti's killers to justice, and I'm willing to pay the price, whatever it takes."

I reached over McSweeny's body and shook Whyte's hand. "It's been good working with you, Hank. Maybe next time we could skip the wrongful arrest. Can you do me one more favour?"

"Name it."

"Let Cosmo out of the tank before you burn the place down," I said. "He didn't ask to be involved in any of this."

He furrowed his brow and unlocked the door. "Sure. Whatever you say, Marlowe."

"It's been a slice." I clapped him on the shoulder and peeked into the hallway. "Take care of yourself."

"Knock 'em dead, Bubbles."

I grinned at him. "Now that's a promise I can keep."

CHAPTER 19

Whyte cracked the door open and I slipped outside. Not a mouse breathed in the security station. The hall outside the interrogation room was cold and white and empty. But the moment I stepped into the hall, a blood-curdling scream erupted at my back. McSweeny writhed on the ground and grabbed for Whyte's leg, his eyes bulging.

Whyte stomped on his hand and growled at me. "Go!"

He slammed the door and I heard it lock behind me. Two security guards appeared at the end of the hallway from the direction of the exit, checking on the noise, but when they saw me in my powder-blue uniform, they relaxed and disappeared around the corner again. I walked as calmly as I could toward the front desk, carrying the briefcase with my backpack in my upgrade hand. I kept my shoulders back and that look of cool indifference on my face which most men found so off-putting. Then I crossed my fingers and hoped that the intake officers were both men.

The *Island Dreamer*'s holding cells were a bit like a vacation themselves compared to the dim, rusted grey cubes of the HoloCity lock up. HCPD loved to kick a man when he was down. Literally, of course, but any time they could dig a heel into the morale of some Grit punk and make sure he knew exactly who he was and where he was going, they made a party of it. From body lice in the bedding to backed-up toilets to overcrowded cells, a bit in the big house was guaranteed to send any person's self-respect on a permanent holiday. Locking up Dreamers looked a lot like the HoloPop adverts for Rae's favourite spa. Just so long as McSweeny wasn't going to sign you up for everlasting meditation.

The heels of my boots clicked as I walked down the hall past the glass walls of empty cells. Besides me and Cosmo, the pen was clean, though I supposed by the end of a week-long cruise it would hold its share of drunks, pinches, and high-cush rabble-rousers on the glow-down. A nice quiet place to get their heads right before they dove headlong into the throng again. I wondered if my Lucky Bastard winnings came with their own clubhouse in the cooler. McSweeny probably cheated me out of that too. In the silence, my heart beat like a drum in my ears, and the clicking of my heels seemed to reverberate down to my very bones. The place was as silent as a tomb and had about as much panache. Sweat trickled between my shoulder blades. I kept the pace down, counting under my breath as I went.

As I passed Cosmo's holding cell, he bugged his eye at me and cocked his hip accusingly. I held up a finger as I passed, assuming Whyte would make good on his promise. I had McSweeny's key card, but the cells looked to have biometric scanners outside too. I passed his unit without turning my head. I was almost to the end of the hall when a door clanged open behind me and shouts rang out. I risked a glance over my shoulder and saw a pair of patrollers opening the door to the interrogation room. I didn't stick around to watch the play. I ran.

Turning the corner toward the front desk, I crashed into the pair of guards I'd seen earlier, crouched on the ground like a couple of rats waiting to pounce on a poor, unsuspecting alley cat. I clobbered one with the hard-shelled briefcase and knocked him flat. The other, a woman with squinty little eyes and a pug nose, barked to alert her pals. Then she clocked me in the side of the head with a right hook that might have knocked a filling loose if I could afford dental work. I let her have a taste of my bougie upgrade and didn't feel too bad when she cracked her head on the floor for good measure.

More shouting from behind me. I could hear Whyte's voice, but I couldn't tell what he was saying. Sounded like a scuffle, which didn't bode well for Whyte. Or me, for that matter. I made a break for the sliding glass doors on the other side of the intake desk and stopped short.

A massive 'gram of the admiral's glowering mug hovered in the middle of the reception area. He frowned gently. "Not quite as cut and dry as I was promised, but we'll see how it unfolds. Whose side are you playing for, Marlowe?"

I didn't bother with the formalities. I flipped him a finger and ran through the projection, sliding through the autodoors as they skimmed sideways on their tracks. On my way out, I hit the big red emergency button next to the exit. An alarm blared and boots pounded behind me, but once the door closed it wasn't going to open again until someone official keyed in the override. I hoofed it out of the security station, barely noticing the blip of the hologram as I exited the camouflaged area, and into the crowd.

Bodies parted for me, and surprised faces turned to watch, but McSweeny's uniform bought me enough room to huff and puff my way to the nearest elevator. I held up the badge pinned to my chest and cleared out the box before I jumped in and keyed in my destination. So far, so good. I had a feeling I knew where the Rose might be staying. Even if Hank was too preoccupied with the coup of his forces to send me the map, I might be able to stumble my way in the right direction. But first, I had to ditch the security uniform and set my affairs in order.

The elevator pinged and opened into the blank-looking hallway I had first found myself in only a few hours earlier. It never ceased to amaze me how quickly things can go from bad to worse to terminal. Maybe I had a knack for self-destruction. I tried to remember where I had stood to open the door to my room and strode slowly down the hall, pausing at intervals, and waiting for the musical chime to signal that I'd found the Lucky Bastard suite once again. I walked much farther down the hall than I thought I should before a little jingle made me stop. The holoscreen dissolved to reveal the tiny lift to my quarters. I looked both ways to make sure I hadn't been followed and slipped inside.

The little elevator hummed silently through my feet as it hoisted me into the upper echelons of the ship. A wave of exhaustion hit me in the sudden quiet and relative safety of the moment. When the door pinged open, I stepped into the suite and relief flooded through every cell of my body.

"You're here."

Hammett glared up at me from the long-haired rug in front of the circus bed. "Where have you been? I've been worried sick."

"I'll fill you in when we get home, okay, bud?"

"You left me alone down there," the little pig squealed indignantly. "After I won all those prizes and everything."

"I was a little busy getting arrested, Ham." I stripped off the hideous blue uniform and dug through my backpack. I paused. "What prizes?"

"You did say I could use the Lucky Bastard Game Room credits."

I tugged the white jumpsuit out of my backpack and my visilenses fell at my feet. I picked them up and put them on my head and reinserted the tubes. "You won?"

"The Boutique Bonanza!" Hammett pranced around the bed to a pile of intricately wrapped boxes and baskets. "No holocreds though, sorry."

"What in the name of Origin is all of this?" I stood in a daze before the mound of luxury goods, any one of which would pay for my rent for a year.

"I don't know," Hammett said. "I can't open them. But this one smells strange."

The pig nosed at a small silver box. I picked it up carefully and lifted the lid. A silver choker sat inside on a soft white cloud of synthetic fluff that glittered gently in the light. A tear-shaped red jewel glinted up at me like a drop of blood. I tilted the box toward the light. The redness of the stone shifted, revealing a sliver of clear glass on one side. I tipped it to the other side and the red liquid inside tilted with my movement. With the tip of my finger, I lifted the jewel away from the metal of the choker collar. A tiny imperfection on the back of the stone was the only visible clue that the necklace was more than a pretty piece of jewellery.

"Be careful, Bubbles." Hammett craned to watch me. "I get a code yellow contamination warning from that one. Undetermined pollutant."

"Was there one of these in the room before we left?" I wondered allowed. "Whyte said all the Platinum Package guests received one."

"If there was, I never sensed it," Hammett said. "Not like this one."

"Still think I'd look good with some high-cush decals?" I

asked, tilting the choker toward the pig.

Hammett shivered theatrically and stomped a hoof. "I'm sorry, okay. Anything but that."

"The Patti simulation at the beach gave me a necklace just like this," I said. "It gave my arm a jolt and disappeared when the simulation ended. Could it have been a warning?"

"Could have been a data transfer," Hammett said. "The more sophisticated simulations can use nanoparticles as a kind of memory storage. But it's locked tech. You need special Trade Zone clearance to use stuff like that."

"Or you need to know how to work around Trade Zone clearances without getting caught," I said. "How difficult would that be?"

"Not impossible," Hammett said. "But almost."

I shrugged my shoulders and put the lid back on the box. I put the box in my bag. "Okay, we'll deal with that later. What else have you got? Any boutique clothing in there?"

"Just wait until you see." Hammett's eyes twinkled with little simulated stars. "Thermonuclear Threads let me choose the prize package option. You owe me big time for this, Miss Marlowe."

The pig buried its holoskinned head into the mountain of gifts and wiggled its tail. I shifted through the loot until I found the one Hammett was so excited about. I hauled a long box up onto the bed and unwrapped the iridescent, recycled-plastic wrapping. I lifted the lid of the box and gasped.

Inside was a full suit of carbon-threaded mesh body armour. High-cush techheads loved units like this. Figured it gave them street cred to be almost bulletproof. Thermonuclear Threads specialized in armour rigs that looked like something out of a medieval fantasy epic or some kind of retro-futurist cyberpunk RPG. Hammett had chosen the proline, the only set of T-Threads specifically designed not to be seen. The invisible armour mesh was preferred by highbinder politicians, celebrities, and drug lords who wanted to appear nonchalant in the face of skyrocketing public executions and high-profile kidnapping stunts. With it, I'd be invulnerable to anything but a clean head shot.

"I had them make alterations to fit your upgrade." Hammett flashed its pearly whites at me. "Come on, try it on."

I bent down and picked up the metallic sphere of the Smart-Pet's real body and hugged it. Hammett's skin tickled wherever it touched mine, and the pig giggled. "You're the best, Ham. You might have saved my bacon."

"I really must insist that you stop using that word." Hammett pushed back at me with a little more electromagnetic force, and I put the pig back on the ground. "It's demeaning and more than a little predatory."

"If we survive to see tomorrow, I promise to book you into therapy."

Hammett huffed. "Are you in trouble again?"

"More like, still," I said and patted the pig on the head. "I need you to send a couple of encrypted messages for me and then take a nap to finish those updates."

I transferred Hammett the files over a short-range, wireless connection that I had to pay a subscription for. It was the first time I'd ever used it, but if my plan worked, it would pay for itself a thousand times over. Granted, in order for it to work, I would have to rely on more than my fair share of Lady Luck's attention. Might be I was just paying to make the post-mortem report a little easier on the desk jockeys.

I pulled on my T-Thread mesh and my white body suit, gave my arm a few tests swings, and slung my bag over my shoulder. Then I rummaged through the pile of Hammett's winnings and snagged a can of NRG to go.

"You know, one of these days you're going to have to try organic calories," Hammett said.

"Maybe," I said. "But today is not that day. Wish me luck, Smarty Pig. The fate of your future dongles depends on it."

"You could get yourself a nice desk job somewhere," the pig grumbled and clip-clopped toward the closet.

"I'd never have been able to afford a trip like this selling digital insurance packages on holohomes," I said. "Enjoy it while it lasts."

"Eight hours and counting." Hammett snorted, and its charging station sing-songed a little jingle. "Maybe next time we can try for half a day."

"Hey, you got to wear a cute new suit and engage in sinfully self-indulgent human vices." I bowed and backed through the holoscreen into the lift. "I spoil you."

Hammett's station chimed as the SmartPet once again entered maintenance mode. But not before one last short-wave transmission hit my tubes. "A small consolation if I end up in a hockmarket parts bin."

CHAPTER 20

I stepped out of the lift, through the holoscreen, and ran straight into Cosmo Régale. He bounced off me, tripped over his platforms, and landed hard on his sparkly tuchus in all his ephemeral glory.

"Son of a skink." He scrabbled back onto his feet like an infant glitter pony learning how to walk. "Where in the whatnow did you come from?"

Then his eyes widened, and he wiggle his unadorned fingers at me. "It's you!"

"It's me," I said. "And it's you. Whyte let you go?"

Cosmo ran a hand over the top of his micro-mohawk. "Well …"

"Is he okay?"

"There was a bit of a kerfuffle," Cosmo brushed some imaginary dust off his skin-tight bodysuit. "Fists were thrown, blasters were blasted, buttons were pressed, you know? I didn't really stick around to find out how it ended. Whyte gave me this before they cuffed him. Analogue, you know?"

He thrust a tube of rolled up paper toward me. I said, "How'd you get away?"

"The usual." He stood with his hip knocked so far to one side I thought he might have broken his leg in the tumble. "'Never mind the fruitcake,' and 'Let's see how far he can go on those gangly getaway sticks,' you know? By the time they realized the fruitcake was flying coop, I was long gone. What is it about glitter that makes people think you're a ninny?"

"Lack of imagination," I said. "Thanks, Cosmo. I owe you one."

"We'll call it even. I did get us tossed in the lockbox, you know?"

I crouched on the ground and flattened the paper as best I could. It appeared to be a blueprint of the cargo bay. But in the centre, a square of static-like markings obliterated half of the central drawing. I scanned the mark with my tattler and got a low-tech, 2D map scan overlay for my visilenses. It was no blinking arrow, but it would do the trick. Whyte had left me a little note in the top right corner of the screen.

"The weather's about to get real ugly around here, Cosmo," I said. "If a guy needed to take cover from the storm, he might do worse than Cargo Bay D2."

The man blinked his white-shadowed eyes at me once. Twice. He smoothed his left eyebrow with a long, unvarnished fingernail and squared his shoulders. "I'll do that. Thank you."

"Can I ask you something?"

"Do I need a lawyer?"

"Why don't you paint your fingernails?"

Cosmo's glittered, pink lips curled, and he looked me up and down as if I was some kind of mutated crustacean that just washed up on his beach blanket. "We're friends, so I'm going to let that slide."

"C'mon, it's been eating at me. What gives? You're glitter from toenails to testicles, but nothing on the digits? I'm about to go get myself in some serious trouble. I can't die with this hanging over my head."

"Who told you about my—" Cosmo narrowed his eyes and turned a galactic cheek at me. "You know what? No. Friends or not, I can't let you get away with this slander. Don't be dazzled by my razzle, sister. I'm all man. And men do *not* paint their finger-nails. Not in this day and age."

"But Cosmo Cosmetics doesn't even have a polish line. I've looked. What about the rest of us? You're forcing your fans right into the arms of Lorena Val—"

Cosmo lunged for me and pressed my lips closed with a single unadorned finger. His eyes brimmed with pain. "Don't say it."

I took his hand in mine and held it. "It's okay. You can tell me."

"I can't compete with her formula," he whispered, tears brimming beneath his pearly lids. "I've tried everything. I cannot bear to release anything … subpar. And I'd rather go naked than wear her line."

"That's it?"

He slapped my shoulder. "*It*?! That's *it*? That's *only* my most embarrassing secret. I've entrusted it to you in the hopes that it will die with you, when you—" He made a fluttering motion with his fingers.

I scanned the map overlay, balled up the paper, and threw it at his head. "Thanks for the vote of confidence."

"Your words, not mine."

"Good luck with your merchandise, friend." I started off down the hallway. "Don't trip on any more dead bodies."

"Wait! Pinky, wait. You weren't serious, were you? I didn't mean it. It was playful banter, you know? The ladies love that. What are you doing?"

"I wish I knew, Cosmo." I turned a corner where the map told me there was no corner and slipped behind another holoscreen.

Cosmo's heels clicked behind me with sudden urgency. He poked his head through the wall. "Where'd you go?"

"Don't stand too close," I said. "This is going to get messy."

A network of narrow passageways branched out and twisted away from the false wall, all painted in a subtle shade of pearly pink. Somewhere down one of the hallways, someone whimpered quietly.

"Is that—"

This time I hushed him with a finger to the lips. He pursed them at me and clenched his jaw, but said nothing. The crying came from a corridor to the right. We tiptoed that way. The pink walls were made of some kind of industrial-grade meringue that absorbed sound like a pillow over a snoring partner's schnozzle. The whimpering was faint, but if we could hear it at all, it must be nearby. I held my breath as we got closer. Sliding my hand along the wall, I felt for any hidden doors that might not be marked on my map. Cosmo followed my lead on the other side. My heart hummed in my chest a little too loudly to be helpful.

Suddenly Cosmo's arm slipped through the wall and he made an excited peeping noise before slapping a hand over his mouth and bugging out his eyes at me. The whimpering stopped. My map didn't have any storage closets or staff facilities listed here. Just a long pink hallway leading toward the hidden mecca of the Last Humanists aboard *Island Dreamer*, and their leader, the Rose. Where were all the pink-robed acolytes? Had they been dispersed throughout the ship, ready to do the Rose's bidding when the time was right? It was too early to tell yet which side the Rose was playing for. I was probably just collateral damage in his vendetta against Swain. But there was always a chance that Swain really was just a sweet potato, and we had a much bigger problem on our hands.

I took a deep breath and ducked my head through the wall. I let the breath out slowly, with bile burning the back of my throat. Dim, red emergency lighting illuminated a scene from a horror flick. Bodies in pink robes stacked up against every wall, like folding chairs in the church basement awaiting the next potluck dinner. Black faces with dead eyes stared up at the ceiling in uniform oblivion. Fingers curled in palms and knees and elbows sagged like dolls' limbs. Necks bent sideways. I'd tossed around the "cult" label, but I didn't think it went this far.

Were the anti-tech weirdos really a death cult in disguise? I hadn't pegged the Last Humanists for this kind of blow down.

The whimpering started again, and Cosmo's face hovered next to mine. His bottom lip trembled but he kept it quiet this time. His eyes popped with the effort, and he looked at me like I was supposed to do something about it. I lifted my upgrade out in front of me and leaned farther into the room. "Is someone there?"

A loud sniff. Then a sound like plastic bags rubbing together. A voice hissed from somewhere to my left. "Bubbles?"

"Dickie?!" I rushed into the room, peering between the rows of bare legs poking out beneath pink robes. "Is that you? What the—"

Dickie Roh, minus his Homburg and plus a shiny silver body bag wrapping around his legs and torso like an ill-fitting tube dress, wriggled out from beneath a bench piled with pink-robed bodies. The bag reflected the red light ominously. A piece of duct tape sagged off his mouth, looking like it had taken whatever few strands of facial hair Dickie had managed to grow with it. He had a welt or two on his brain box, not bigger than apples but enough to give me a headache just looking at them. He managed to focus his dark brown eyes in my direction and whimpered again. "I knew you would find me."

"How long have you been here, Dickie?" I knelt and ripped the last of the tape away, leaving behind a raised pink patch of freshly depilated skin.

Dickie squealed and twisted away from me. "There goes six months of my masculinity, you boob!"

Cosmo's platform shoes tiptoed up beside me. He whispered, "What the cuss is going on here?"

"God?" Dickie's eyes watered. "Oh no. I'm dead, aren't I? Are you dead, too, Bubbles? They told me they were going to kill you. I thought—"

"You are not dead." I rolled Dickie onto his face and tugged at the body bag. "Unlike the company you keep. Who said they were going to kill me?"

"They aren't dead, Bubbles." Dickie shrugged out a shoulder and an arm and started helping me peel the crinkly silver material from his body, his eyes as wide as blaster barrels and just as jumpy. "They're plugs. All of them. High-end, illegal, AI plugs. Flesh skins and everything."

237

"Robots?" I grabbed Dickie by the collar and shook him harder than I meant to. "Are you sure?"

"Every last one of them, except—" His eyes roved over my shoulder, staring into the darkness behind me. Ice prickled across my shoulder blades. "I don't know, I thought I heard someone else struggling when they dropped me. Then they topped me. I didn't see what happened to her."

"What the shiznat is a flesh skin?" Cosmo stomped the floor next to me. "Like they use in those Porno flicks?"

"Those aren't real." Dickie extricated himself from the rest of the material and crept between the lifeless, pink-robed bodies. "I mean, they were, like, eons ago. OE tech. But flesh skins have been illegal for hundreds of years. Ever since AIs got sophisticated enough to mimic human speech patterns and behaviours. The Trade District only allows AIs housed within TD approved shells."

"Tell that to the gearheads on this cruiser." I shadowed Dickie as he peered into a darkened corner. "Human holoskins are a dime a dozen."

"Holoskins, yeah?" Dickie crawled on the ground between two rows of acolyte robots, and I felt my own skin crawl away in the opposite direction. "Not flesh skins. These are different. Cut them and they bleed synthetic blood. You can't tell one from your first-grade teacher unless you open them up. Which we frown upon in case it actually is your first-grade teacher. That's why it's banned tech. Holoskins can be scanned. There are fail-safes built into their designs. The idea is to prevent people from using robots to do their dirty work."

Cosmo crossed his arms over his narrow chest and shuffled back to the holoscreened doorway. "Or from becoming their dirty workers."

"Did you say cruiser?" Dickie smacked his head on something and cursed. "Where exactly are we?"

"Orbiting Terra Firma on the *Island Dreamer*," I said. "The Lucky Bastard Sweepstakes seems to have been less lucky and more fu—"

"So much for luxury cruising," Dickie said. "I wonder if the concussions are free, or if I'm getting a bill to go with the lumps."

"What's wrong with these plugs," I asked. "Are they listening to us right now?"

"I don't think so," Dickie said from somewhere underneath a bench. "I think they're, like, on standby or something. Here."

He tugged something shiny and silver out into the dim light of the emergency pulsers. He pulled back the cover of the body bag and revealed a mop of curly, black hair clinging to her fine brown skin. The woman's wide black eyes shot from side to side, and her nostrils flared as she sucked air in and out over top of the dull grey tape across her mouth. I pulled the tape away slowly, and she gasped in huge breaths.

"Sure, you're all gentle with her," Dickie said. "She's not even trying to grow a moustache."

I wiped the hair away from her face while she started to relax. She didn't quite look like the 'gram Whyte had shown me, but I had to ask. "Patti?"

Her eyes darted to my face and her chest rose and fell, rose and fell. She licked her lips. "Who are you?"

"My name is Bubbles Marlowe," I said. "Do you remember me?"

"No, I—" She shook her head. "I don't remember… I feel strange. How long have I been here?"

"Dickie?"

"I don't know." Dickie ran a hand through his dark hair and let out a long breath. "The last thing I remember is recovering from that curry cart lunch after we sealed up the documents on that divorce case."

"That was over a week ago."

"Well, I did get hit on the head a few times." He crouched next to Patti and rubbed the back of his skull. "Cut me some slack."

"You don't remember anything about the Lucky Bastard Sweepstakes?" I asked. "Or making my business cards?"

"You don't have business cards," Dickie said. "Terrible move in this industry. Everyone has cards."

"I just spoke to you this morning." I ran a hand over my face, trying to make the pieces fit without jamming them together too hard. "Or was it yesterday morning?"

"Nope." Dickie frowned. "Can't have. I get food and water once a day, and toilet privileges twice, plus the complimentary sapping. I mean, it blends together a bit, what with all the knocks to the noodle, but I've been up here for days. Can't say for sure about her."

"This is bad, Dickie." I shook my head. "It was you. I would have sworn it. How could a robot mimic your . . . quirks ... so perfectly."

"Well, I'm no expert. But who knows who monitors our tattlers. Just because the Trade Zone says its illegal doesn't mean nobody does it. They could have years worth of audio and video data to run through the AI programming. Oh man. Feed searches?" Dickie's eyes went wide.

"What about you, Patti?" I said.

"I don't remember anything since the lab," Patti said. "Jimi—"

I turned to her. "What about Jimi?"

"He was hurt," she whispered. "Someone had ... I called it in ..."

"So, either the Dickie in my office is one of these plugs"—I grabbed Dickie's right arm and twisted it behind his back, knocking him to his knees—"or you are."

"Ow! Hey! Not me," he said. "Definitely not me."

"How do I know for sure?"

"I'm going to wet my pants if you twist that arm any harder,"

Dickie said. "That's a pretty sure sign."

"Go take a leak." I shoved him away from me. "Cosmo, watch him."

"Girl, that is not my scene."

"You're going to be travelling with him," I said. "You might want to know if he's a robot."

"It's okay, man." Dickie picked himself up off the floor and shook one leg like he was warming up for a sprint. "There's not much to see. But what I lack in size I make up for with unbridled enthusiasm."

Cosmo rolled his eyes and followed Dickie to a far corner of the room.

"Where are we?" the woman asked, turning her dark eyes on me. A silver strap slipped off her shoulder.

"On the *Island Dreamer*."

"Hank," she said. "Is he okay?"

"More or less," I said. "Except he thinks you're dead."

"I never meant to hurt him." Her voice trembled and her eyelashes glittered as if with tears. "Everything we were trying to do. It's all got twisted."

"You definitely don't remember hiring me?"

"To do what?" She wiped at her dry eyes and started to crawl out of the bag. "I don't even know who you are."

"I'm a private investigator." I helped her to her feet. She

242

was barefoot. Tiny. Barely tall enough to see over my shoulder. "A couple days ago I had a call from a client who was looking for a woman matching your description. She had a message to deliver."

"What message?"

"Mama wants the drop."

Fear washed over her expression like night falling on a city; she shimmered sharper and brighter. She reached out and grabbed my arm with a child-sized hand. "Mama wants …"

Then she stepped back with a hand over her mouth. She whispered, "The choker."

I swung my bag around to the front and opened it, digging through the rumpled contents until I found the box. I brought it out and flipped the lid open with one hand. "Is this it?"

Patti Whyte shrieked and stumbled backward. She knocked into one of the pink-robed plugs and fell sideways, crashing onto her right hip and hand. The body fell on top of her and she struggled under its weight. The acolyte rolled, and an arm flopped to one side, hitting the floor with a dull thud. Its dead eyes stared at the ceiling as if they were made of glass. Patti managed to get herself out from under the thing and scrambled over it like a wild animal.

"Get it away from me," she screamed. Her white-rimmed eyes danced frantically around the room. But the way she stared at me, I knew it wasn't the bodies she was afraid of.

CHAPTER 21

Cosmo appeared at my shoulder. "What's the ruckus? Why are you scaring the poor thing?"

"It's not me," I said. "It's the necklace."

"Oh, those things." Cosmo slapped the lid closed again. "Fashion tragedy of the decade. Just give it a week. Hardly worth screaming over."

"Where did you get that?" Patti asked.

"They're all over the ship," I said. "You—or someone who looks like you—ordered them for all the Platinum Package guest rooms."

Patti shook her head. "I would never ..."

"That's a relief," Cosmo said. "The girl has some sense,

although I don't know about the Shoeless Josephine thing. Speaking of relief, your friend appears to be human"—he waved a hand in front of his face—"and very dehydrated. His story checks out."

"Good," I said. "I need you to take these two away from here. They need to lie low. Set them up in your room."

Cosmo clapped his hands. "We can do make-overs!"

"Can you make me blond?" Dickie called from over by the door. "I always thought I should have been born blond."

"Honey, I can make you anything you want to be." Cosmo picked his way carefully over the pile of scattered bots and stood next to Dickie. "Can we go now? This place gives me the hee-bie-jeebies."

"No," Patti said. "I have to contact the Rose. There's been a terrible mistake."

"What a coincidence," I said. "That's where I'm headed. I've got some questions I need answered, and I think he is the only—"

"The Rose is here?" Her voice tickled with something like horror. "On this ship?"

"That's what I've been led to believe."

"We'll just be going then," Cosmo said. "I remember the way out. We'll meet you on the strip after I liberate my merchandise"—he turned to Dickie—"how do you feel about breaking and entering?"

Dickie shrugged. "I'll try anything twice."

I turned and motioned for them to move. Dickie looked over his shoulder and lifted a hand, then stopped. His jaw fell open. Cosmo's eyes widened. He slapped a hand over his glitter pink lips. A high-pitched noise escaped.

"Uh, Bubbles," Dickie said. "You might want to—"

I spun around and lifted my upgrade to protect my head. Something whipped past my face, making the air sing. And twice I flinched back and caught a blow on my forearm. A pink-robed acolyte stood between Patti and me, another stood behind her with an arm wrapped around Patti's throat. Others were stirring. I shoved back on my attacker, but he didn't stumble. He—it— smiled.

"You will all be coming with us," the android said in a perfectly human voice. "Don't waste time fighting. You will only tire yourself. The Rose wants you in shipshape, at least for your interview."

A pink-robed army lifted itself off the floors and benches of the storage room, moving as a unit. It would be pointless to resist. Patti's eyes bulged, and her fingers clawed uselessly at the pale arm of her captor.

"You might want to let her breathe," I said.

The plug loosened its grip slightly, and Patti wheezed. One of the acolytes stepped forward and directed me toward the door. I turned. Dickie and Cosmo were wrapped in some kind of netting. Two pink soldiers moved in unison to pick the men up and sling them over their shoulders. I swallowed as Dickie and

Cosmo were carried out the door, followed by a unit of eight more android acolytes.

Something hard hit me in the small of my back, and I took a step toward the door. Only the faint rustling of robes betrayed the fact that another twenty or so of the robots were moving into formation behind me. I was marched through the holoscreen and into the meringue-coated corridor outside. Once I emerged, the preceding unit fell into step ahead of me. I glanced once over my shoulder to make sure Patti was okay. She, too, was slung over the shoulder of one of the acolytes. I half expected to be picked up myself, but they made me walk. Maybe it was my lucky day. Or maybe they were wary of the upgrade.

Our strange procession marched through the maze of corridors. I followed our progress on my visilens map. We buzzed straight to the bud at the centre of the flower, like busy little bees. I wondered if the Last Humanist Church in HoloCity followed a similarly twisted floor plan. It was kind of fascinating, even if the Rose had some strange ideas about hospitality. The purity of the species, too, while we were on the topic. Maybe Swain wasn't so bad after all. At least he just traded in the usual human vices.

We followed the corridors in what felt like a convoluted spiral. Once we'd wound ourselves toward the centre of the maze, the soldiers fell back, lining the corridor on either side ahead of me. The two acolytes that held my friends stood before a door. It looked like the petals of an enormous flower folded in on themselves. I approached behind them. The acolyte who had been prodding me stepped to my left, and the one carrying Patti appeared to my right. The layered panels of the door shifted and fell back like a flower opening itself to the sun. From inside, a blindingly bright light spilled into the corridor.

I followed the soldiers inside.

The room was filled with a stepped dais, atop of which a pale-pink throne made of iridescent petals bloomed against a curved wall that seemed to glow with starlight. A figure, blurred against the light, perched atop the throne in perfect stillness.

Swain was there. His body draped over the steps like a dingy bit of old carpeting. A dark stain spread from his body and dripped off the steps into a puddle on the floor. The soldiers in front of me dropped Dickie and Cosmo like sacks of laundry, and the sacks grunted but lay still. The soldiers stepped back to guard the door.

"Greetings," said a soft voice, neither kind nor unkind, male nor female. "We wondered how long it would take before you joined us."

"I didn't intend to join," I said. "Cults aren't really my bag."

"And yet you are here," the voice said. "With us."

"I'm here, anyway," I said. "Bit late to the party, I guess. When did Swain get here?"

"The fool bribed the admiral in order to hitch a ride on our bangtail." Bell-like laughter rippled through the air from the dais. The voice raised the hairs on the back of my neck. "Isn't that just too perfect?"

"All that planning for nothing, huh?"

"You are a difficult woman to guide, Betty 'Bubbles' Marlowe. We laid many paths to direct you here. It is always interesting to see which tiny flecks of pollen attract which bees. It says much about a person."

I clenched my cybernetic fist and wished again that I hadn't sworn off firearms. "And what have you learned about me?"

"Swain was attracted to power," the voice said. "Being the Chief of Police only gave him a taste of it, and he wanted more. Like a snake, he wriggled his way to the top of the HoloCity rubbish heap and crowned himself king."

"Seems a little hard on snakes." I twitched a finger and my tattler started pinging like mad. A news feedreel scrolled quickly by until I killed it with a button. "Sorry, I don't really know how to use this thing yet."

"We know exactly how to use men like Swain." The speaker on the dais ignored me completely, revelling in their own brilliance, I supposed. I let them talk. "The admiral likes to pull strings just to watch the puppets dance. He wasn't difficult either. And Patti Whyte just wants to save the world. Isn't that right, Patti?"

A muffled noise came from behind my shoulder, then a thump. I didn't look back. Patti struggled her way to her feet and said, "That's what we all want."

"We do, my child. We do. And you have done well. You will

be rewarded."

Patti stepped past me and climbed the dais in her bare feet, slipping past Swain and the blood, to kneel before the Rose. She stayed like that. As still as a glittering silver stone. My stomach sank.

"You called me to find the girl in the silver dress?" I said. "Why?"

"Punch Blanco called the admiral. But you know all about Punch, don't you?"

"Punch Blanco doesn't exist," I said. "That doesn't answer my question. Why bring me in on it?"

"We needed someone competent, who would not be swayed by corruption." The Rose stood against a halo of light and stepped down the dais toward me, past Patti, like an angel descending from heaven. Long, narrow feet, bare and pale in the light, came into view first. Then the long Last Humanist robes trailed behind like a river of pink satin, spilling down the steps after them. "Someone motivated by human suffering above all else."

My eyes fell on Swain's corpse. "Needed me for what?"

"To stop him." The Rose's torso, narrow shoulders, and small breasts with collar bones like daggers, slipped out of the blinding halo of light. Then her face, as calm and expressionless as the moon, came into view, surrounded by a crown of white-blonde hair.

"You're a woman," I said.

251

"Am I?" She smiled at me. "Swain knew about our formula. A nootropic of this magnitude would be a powerful bartering chip to a man like him. In the right circles—the drug syndicates, the highbinder politicians, the trade barons—it would be invaluable."

"If not for the side effects."

"That's right." She smiled wider, perfectly white teeth in a perfectly white face. "Swain's eagerness got the best of him. He flooded the market with a deadly drug. And the city licked it up. Every last drop."

"That's what you wanted all along." I relaxed my nerves and let my arm fall limp beside me. "Patti wasn't trying to stop the delivery at all. She was trying to draw Swain's attention to it."

"The Purification of HoloCity," the Rose said. "Swain opened the gates for the first wave. And the second wave—"

"Starts here," I finished. "With the necklaces. What's in them?"

"Your friend Jimi made a very significant discovery," the Rose frowned. "A brilliant human mind, unfortunately contaminated. Tropical Punch is exactly what we intended it to be. Jimi wanted to remove the secret ingredient. A tiny thing, really. Microscopic."

"A virus," I said.

The Rose laughed suddenly, a musical trill that lifted the hairs on the back of my neck and made my bowels turn to water. "Patti told me you were primitive."

"What then?"

"Particulate intelligence," she said. "Nanoids. It's perfect, really. We can eliminate bodies contaminated with incompatible tech and turn pure bodies into vessels for the Spirit of Humanity, vehicles to aid the second wave of Purification."

"The girl who attacked me in the casino," I said. "You were controlling her?"

Her and how many others? Whyte, for one…

"People have become so fond of technological contaminants." The Rose frowned. "They hardly notice when they're receiving outside inputs anymore. The fools think every thought that pops into their heads originates with them. As if we haven't been manipulating the human mind via social norms and media representation for millennia."

"So, the Last Humanist Church is, what?" I turned my wrist toward the Rose in all her radiant purity. "And end-of-days cult?"

"Don't be simple, child." The Rose turned her heavenly face toward me, and her expression hardened. "Terra Firma has millions of solar rotations ahead of it. Such a human presumption, to believe that the end of you will be the end of everything. No. There is so much more in store."

"What are you, then, if not human?"

"I am the last of the Last Humanists and the first of the New," she said. "Now, you have something that I want."

I took a step backwards. "Me?"

"You don't think I brought you here just to reveal my plans

for world domination, do you? This isn't a comic book." She smiled again. "My techRose operative transferred a file to you. I need it."

"Your operative was dead when I got there," I said. "Didn't you get the memo? Your friend Tesla lopped off the poor bunny's head. I thought it was Patti."

"Tesla decommissioned two very expensive AI plugs," the Rose said. "And stole our prototype necklace. But not before you delivered my message, and my operative reciprocated the gesture. I hope it didn't pinch."

My hand wandered to the side of my neck where the skin was still tight and sore.

"Oh. Is that where she hit you?" The Rose cocked her head to one side and smiled again. I was beginning to think she had missed some important social cues as a child. "In that case, I'm afraid you might find the extraction process unpleasant."

Her right hand shot out toward my throat.

CHAPTER 22

Metallic fingernails like knives sliced into my flesh as I twisted away. I grabbed the nearest android in pink and hammered it in the spine with my metal fist. The fabric of the robe tore away with the flesh skin, exposing a pale skeleton of alloyed metal and sparking wire nerves. A blood-like fluid pooled on the ground where the machine fell.

The Rose snarled and lunged again, but Dickie rolled onto his knees and threw himself into her path, sending the First New Humanist sprawling across the dais. "Take that, robo-Rose!"

"Are you okay, Dick?" I hit the button on my arm that released the grapefruit knife and attempted to cut away the strange, sticky fibers of the net binding his arms and legs. Something clobbered me across the shoulders, and I fell on top of Dick with the air knocked out of my lungs. The blow should have broken my back. Then I remembered the mesh armour Hammett had commissioned for me and promised myself I'd buy any new toy in the SmartPet catalogue that the little piggy heart desired if only I could stop being dense for long enough to survive the next fifteen minutes.

I felt the assaulting android approaching from behind and waited until it was just close enough. Using my enhancement for a little extra vertical thrust, I donkey-kicked backward and hit the thing where the groin would be on a human. The man screamed and collapsed on the ground. Oops. The not-a-robot clutched at himself like he was afraid something would fall off and rolled on the ground in agony. Maybe I shouldn't have kicked so hard.

I caught a motion from the corner of my eye, and I spun sideways with my arm up for protection. The pink-robed monster carried a disturbingly human looking arm, torn from one of its fallen comrades and still dripping synthetic blood from wires like tendons. It swung the severed limb in an overhead arc, lunging forward at the same time, and brought the makeshift bludgeon crashing down on top of me.

I covered my head with both arms and felt the blow ricochet across the mesh armour. The impact jarred my joints and ligaments and felt like it bruised every square inch of muscle in my body, but my bones didn't shatter. I considered that a win. I broke the block and swung upward with my cybernetic arm, striking the robot in the chest to send it flying backwards. Scrambling to my feet, I scanned frantically for some kind of weapon. None of the androids appeared to be packing heat, but I didn't think I was going to be able to grab and punch my way out of this one. There were at least thirty more soldiers outside.

The second guard stepped away from the door and into the fray. I crouched low and charged it, hoping the body armour would act like a battering ram if I got going fast enough. I hit the shell with a crunch, but the angle was all wrong. The nerves inside my prosthetic screamed, and I dropped to my knees, cradling my arm.

"Behind you!" Cosmo's high-pitched screech pierced through the fog of pain, and I whipped my head around.

The Rose stalked toward me, limping slightly in her bare feet, with a little pisskicker pointed at my chest. "Now hold still. This will hurt excruciatingly, but only for a little while."

The android I just tackled wrapped its arms around me and held me in a vice-like embrace. The one I'd tossed earlier stood up, its torso twisted at an awkward angle. What would have been a fatal injury to a human appeared to be little more than an inconvenience to the robot. It shuffle-stepped sideways toward us to join the party. Dickie kicked at the Rose's legs again as she passed but this time she was ready for him. She cracked him in the nose with the heel of her foot. Blood spurted from the wound and my partner keeled over backward.

Cosmo whimpered and wriggled himself over to check on Dickie. The android tightened its grip around me, one hand up under my chin, holding my head back to expose my throat. The Rose extended her long, metal claws toward my throat, lifting the little gun as she did, keeping it well out of the reach of my enhancement. The room was silent, but for Cosmo's whimpering and my own ragged breathing. I gritted my teeth, waiting for the gory end to my pathetic life. Staring death in the face, seeing her for what she really was, I felt a little ripped off. Getting my throat opened by a wannabe demigod was a bit of a cop-out after everything I'd been through.

A commotion outside the door broke through the silence and my contemplation. Shouts and gunfire erupted in sharp staccato bursts. The Rose turned her head for a fraction of a second. It was enough. Something leaped on her back. A furious ball of curly black hair and silver sequins clung to the Rose with thin brown limbs wrapped around her waist. The little pisskicker went off and the limping robot went down. Parts needed for reassembly. The android holding me faltered. I broke out of its grip and swung my metal fist backward into its face. A shower of sparks rained down, and I got a good jolt through the prosthetic. I had forgotten about the grapefruit knife.

I spun around, placed a knee on the pink-robed robot's chest, and pushed it off my arm. Shaking out the pins and needles, I flexed my fingers and looked up to see Patti wrap a plasma wire around the Rose's thin white neck.

"Patti, no!" I cried, and I dove for the struggling pair just as the door into the Mezzanine chapel exploded inward and a swarm of grey HCPD uniforms, peppered liberally with Whyte's baby blues, burst onto the scene.

"Everyone put your hands in the air!" The shouting voice was familiar. But it was too late. Momentum was on my side. I hit the Rose in the chest and knocked her backward. We both landed on top of Patti. It wasn't enough to stop her. The wire sizzled as it cut through the religious leader's throat and an ozone stench filled the air mixed with something like damp metal and burnt plastic. The Rose's body spasmed and twitched. Then the skin around the throat melted.

I backed away from the horror, my mouth gaping. Sparks burst out of the wound as the Rose's body kicked one last time and her head rolled off her body. Its head. Its body. The Last Humanist wasn't human at all. Patti shoved the android corpse off herself and stood up, her wild eyes roving around the room. "Hank?"

"Patti," Whyte stumbled forward with cuffs on his wrists and fell to his knees. "Patti, you're all right."

"What have they done to you?" Patti crouched next to her husband and used the coil of wire to cut through his bonds.

"Uh, is that allowed?" One of the HCPD lunks scratched his head.

"Hey, Bubbles," Said a familiar voice from the back of the group. "What's the smoke?"

"Weiland, you desk jockey." I panted, trying to hide the relief in my voice. "What are you trying to do? Make 'Better Late Than Never' the new HCPD force motto?"

"Hey, next time you want my help, try asking for it," Detective Tom Weiland said. "This whole telling me to go lick a duck and then sending me off to get ambushed by an illegal AI plug thing was a little obtuse, even for you."

"To be fair, I didn't know he was a plug when I sent you. I take it you got my message?"

"I tried to report the plug to Chief Swain, but he still wasn't in. After a little snooping around, I found out he'd hopped a bangtail with the idea of arresting you and Punch Blanco in one fell swoop. I put a call in to the admiral and fed him the line you suggested, commandeered a Grit squad, and managed to make the last jump up here."

"So that would be a yes."

"You and Blanco, though. Is there something you'd like to tell me?"

"Many things, Weiland. But none of them are fit for mixed company."

Weiland groaned and ran a thick-fingered hand over his face. "You promised me you weren't going to go digging into—"

"There is no Punch Blanco," Patti said. She was busy nursing Whyte's ego, a performance he was enjoying a little too much. "Blanco was me, in a prototype sim-skin I have been developing for Libra that's undetectable by your helmet cams."

"Didn't stop Swain from trying to arrest him." I pointed to the smear on the pretty white dais. "Turns out Punch Blanco was the sweet spot. I'm a little put out about that after Swain went all the trouble of trying to fade me."

"Ahem. Ahem. AHEM." A bug-eyed, galaxy-painted face peered up from between my boots. "This is a lovely view, sugar. But could you untie me, please? My hands are going numb and without my hands that only leaves my—"

"I'll get it." Weiland elbowed me out of the way and got to work on the nets.

Whyte picked himself up off the floor and wrapped an arm around his no-longer-dead wife. "What was the message to the admiral?" he asked. "I notice it got the HCPD on board, but it didn't get me off the hook."

"I told him the Rose was distributing Blanco's merchandise via those cute little necklaces Patti ordered," I said. "That Swain needed backup, and it wasn't clear who we could trust."

"You could have added a line to clear my name, couldn't you?" Whyte rubbed his wrists and frowned. "I thought I was going to get snuffed when these goons showed up."

I shrugged. "It was mostly true."

"That was a neat trick you did with the news feeds," he said. "We never would have sussed out the Rose's plan without you."

"My trick?" I said. "I didn't do anything."

"You broadcasted the Rose's little acceptance speech to

everyone on the *Island Dreamer*," Weiland said, pulling away the last of the netting around Cosmo's glitter platformed feet. "You didn't do that on purpose? Slick moves, Private Investigator."

"Yeah, that's P.I. not I.T." I flicked on the holoscreen and saw the live feed icon blinking in the corner. I said, "Show's over folks." Then I killed the transmission. The feeds would be buzzing for weeks. I'd have to kill Rae, if I didn't get arrested.

"When I arrived, Whyte had been taken into custody and the admiral wanted all units on finding and helping Swain," Weiland said. "But we couldn't get a pin on him. I figured he had a lead on Blanco and wanted to do the takedown while everyone was arguing about what to do with you. Then your feed starts pinging every tattler on the ship …"

"And the Rose started yapping. We got turned in the right direction pretty quick," Whyte said.

I yawned, suddenly feeling the weight of the last couple of days land on my shoulders like a sack of hockmarket rejects. "Can we save the debriefing for after I take a nap? I think I'm going cross-eyed, here."

"We can debrief anytime you like, baby." Cosmo sidled up to me and wrapped an arm around my waist. "You just say the word."

I collapsed onto the stairs and put my head between my knees. "The word is never, Cosmo."

"Don't worry, man." Weiland snorted. "She's turned down

better men than you."

"I hope you don't mean yourself, meat brick." Cosmo snapped his fingers and sashayed his way toward the exit, high-stepping over the litter of android parts and puddles of fluids. "Because if I were you, I'd worry less about me and more about those eyebrows. They don't call me Cosmo Régale, Destroyer of Masculine Paradigms for nothing. You're just a grey sprinkle on the rainbow cupcake of life, my friend. More disappointing than an unsalted pretzel. Now if you'll excuse me, I have some other trash to take out. Whyte, you sunburnt monkey, where is my security detail? I'm about to show Lorena Valentia the definition of a Grit strip."

We all watched the intergalactic king of glitter strut his way out of the room, his wings torn and drooping, but somehow no-less glorious.

Whyte shot me a look that said a thousand words. "You sure about him?"

"Let it play out." The words felt thick in my mouth. "Can't get any weirder."

Whyte shrugged and sent two of his men to escort Cosmo to the cargo bay. Cosmo glanced one last time over his shoulder and called, "We'll chat after your nap, Pinky. Cosmo's got all the time in the galaxy to wait for you."

"Pinky?" Weiland raised a decidedly ungroomed eyebrow at me.

"Save it, Tom." The room listed a little to one side and some pretty coloured dots did a little dance for me. "Dickie needs a medic and I need …"

I forgot what I needed. I tipped forward and gave the floor a kiss.

Someone cursed and fumbled with my arms and legs. I tried to help them, but none of my body parts seemed to agree about which direction we were pointed, so I stopped fighting and tried to enjoy the ride. I hoped they'd set me up in a class cell this time. Private toilet and everything.

CHAPTER 23

I slept through the next trip on the bangtail and woke up in a hospital with Detective Tom Weiland sitting next to my bed, reading an old pulp novel with one eye and watching me with the other. On the bedside table next to me, a little plastic dish with a red crystal in it sat under a microscope. I glanced from the crystal to Weiland. "Taking a study break?"

Weiland folded the book closed and sat up straight in his chair. "You're awake."

"You're very good," I said. "Ever consider being a detective? I hear the pay sucks, but you work enough hours that you don't really notice."

"I see your sense of humour is still intact."

I tried to push myself up in the bed and realized my prosthetic was missing. "What about the rest of me?"

"Rae came to pick up the prototype," Weiland said. "She said she had some adjustments to make after watching your livestream. I had to give it to her, the papers were in order."

"They always are," I said. "How long have I been here?"

"A couple days," he said. "They dug this thing out of your neck, but I wouldn't let anyone take it away until I'd heard from you exactly what happened. This illegal plug market is a big score. We can't afford to mess it up."

In the smooth, white hospital room Tom Weiland was like a stone giant in his grey uniform. A little door in the far corner housed the toilet and shower facilities. Weiland must have been going elsewhere because it didn't look like he'd fit through the narrow doorway. He took up more than his fair share of the space in the main room. He'd have been breathing up all my air if he'd been breathing. But he seemed to forget about that as he pondered his case.

"What have you got so far?"

"The acolytes have all been scanned, and the plugs decommissioned. The Last Humanist ranks aren't nearly so impressive without the robo-mystics. We interviewed Hank and Patti Whyte," he said. "Patti's story checks out. She was a scientist at Libra, working undercover for the Last Humanists. She saw it as her spiritual calling. The nootropic in Tropical Punch was her baby. She thought she was going to expand the potential of the human species. Save the world. But Jimi Ng noticed a flaw in the formula. The nanoids. Patti knew she hadn't put them there, and she suspected sabotage by Libra. She used the Punch Blanco skin to attempt to intercept Tesla's delivery—"

"What happened to Tesla? I was sure he'd be on the *Island Dreamer*."

"We found his plug charging in another storage unit like the one you saved Dickie and Pattie from."

"I'm going to have some serious trust issues because of this case," I said. "I can feel it. I'll need years of therapy before I don't suspect everyone is a robot."

"It would probably do you good." Weiland smirked.

I ignored him. There was something I needed to work out. "So, the real Patti fails to intercept the delivery. But she has this antidote that Jimi created. The Rose is going to send an operative to pick up the new formula. Everything rates until they move too fast on Jimi, and Patti clues in that the Last Humanists don't want the fix, they want to destroy it. She plays it cool, and when the operative drifts in she nails it with the wire—you know, for a tiny woman she packs a serious wallop ... was she the one cutting off droid heads on the cruiser too?"

Weiland shrugged. "This case is like one of those funhouse attractions; you think you know where you're going until you hit a wall that looks like a mirror. Nothing is what it seems to be."

"'Galaxies, like the hoary breath of long-dead gods' ..."

Weiland rolled the book in his big hands and tossed it on the bed. "Getting poetic in your old age?"

"Something I heard once," I said. "Makes me wonder. We have our rules, and the Last Humanists have theirs. This tech is only illegal because we say it is, right? We have no way of knowing how sophisticated these machines have become. Maybe we're the old gods, not dead yet but taking our last breaths."

"You going to join the church?"

"I'm too old-school to be compatible with the software upgrades." I yawned. "These riddles are making my brain hurt."

Weiland pulled an evidence bag out of his pocket, tipped the device in the dish into the bag, and tucked it away. He put his huge hands on his knees and pushed himself up. "I'm going to go get some coffee. Can I get you anything?"

"Coffee would be good," I said and leaned back in my pillow. "Unless they'll let me have a can of NRG."

Weiland shook his head. "Your nutritional profile was so out of whack I thought we were going to have to send you through the android scanners. Maybe I should bring you some fruits and veggies."

"If this is HoloCity General, they can't afford fruits and veggies. I'll have a coffee and a vitamin water if you're so concerned. I'll eat whatever they bring me, I promise."

He moved his bulk away from the bed and pushed the chair under the side table. "Okay."

"Do me a favour, Tom?"

He turned, a small smile playing on his wide mouth. His eyes were a prettier shade of blue than I remembered. "Sure, Bubbles."

"Leave me your gun, would you?" I said. "I feel naked without my prosthetic."

He hesitated a moment, then reached into his standard-issue overcoat. Long and grey, and made to keep the rain out.

"Don't tell the brass." He pulled out his sidearm and tossed in on the bed and turned back for the door. He said, "How do you take your coffee?"

My heart thudded in my ears. I picked up the gun with my right hand, pulled it into my lap, and flicked off the safety with my thumb. I said, "With bubble gum."

Weiland stopped short and turned around with the question knotted up in his eyebrows. "I'm sorry?"

"Me too," I said.

I lifted the gun and pulled the trigger. I was still a fair shot. Old habits die hard. A hole opened like a third eye in Weiland's forehead, and he dropped like a discarded marionette. A little spray of sparks preceded the trickle of synthetic blood, but the arms and legs didn't twitch. Must have hit the CPU. I dropped the gun on my bedsheets and hit the call button.

CHAPTER 24

They found the real Detective Tom Weiland cuffed to his own bedposts, blindfolded, and with his underwear shoved in his mouth. Never put it past the pro skirts. Class jobs or not. I was never going to let him live it down. Once he was sufficiently recovered and had gone through the body scanner to make sure he really was who he thought he was, he visited me at my office.

"I brought coffee," he said, pushing the door open with his hip. "And doughnuts."

"I hope you got her order right." Hammett snorted from under my desk and clip-clopped over to the door. "Last time you forgot how she likes it, she shot you between the eyes."

"Don't worry," Weiland said. "It's mostly sugar. And I

bought the doughnut with the pinkest icing I could find. It even has sprinkles."

I eyed him suspiciously. "Why are you being so nice to me?"

"Because if you hadn't nailed the plug, I'd still be wearing fuzzy handcuffs and a blindfold."

"They were fuzzy?" I took a sip of the coffee. He still remembered. "I wish they'd let me come for the sweep."

"Pink, even."

I raised an eyebrow. "Feeling nostalgic?"

"You never miss the way things used to be?" He sat his bulk down across from me and bit into his doughnut. "It wasn't all bad."

"Nothing ever is," I said. "But that doesn't make it good for you."

"She says while consuming enough sugar to give diabetes to a horse," he said. "Where's your pink upgrade? You're back to the steel-skeleton look, huh?"

"Rae needed to make sure I hadn't broken her baby," I said. I licked some pink icing off my finger and put my feet up on the desk. "Did you track down Patti Whyte?"

He shook his head. "How'd you know she was going to run? By the time you gave us the lead, she was long gone. They found Hank, though."

"Dead?"

"Not yet. But he was so pumped full of the nanoids that the doctors aren't sure they can keep him alive through the decontamination process." He rubbed his face. "Why would she do that?"

"Patti was never human," I said. "Everything about her story was true except for that little detail. And with her knowledge of skins, she can hide in plain sight. We won't find her unless she wants to be found."

"Libra has offered to invest a lot of money into advanced skin detection systems and anti-AI weapons systems. I think the Trade Zone is going to go for it."

"Oh good," I said. "I was just thinking we needed to get this tech into the hands of a Mega-Corporation. Did the Trade Zone stamp an expiration date on the human species or are we just going to give it the sniff test every couple of years?"

"You can't fight the system, Bubbles. HoloCity is a machine of its own making."

"We built it and now it improves itself," I said. "Isn't that right, Ham?"

"Now you're starting to get it." The pig sniffed around Detective Weiland's shoes and then trotted over to me. I picked it up and placed it in my lap. "You're just the fleshy cogs in the gear box. Monkey's in the barrel."

"You'd do well to remember who pays the subscription on your gaming module," I said and scratched the holoskin behind the ears. Hammett grinned up at me with its Chiclet smile.

Weiland gave the pig a baleful look and asked, "How did you know about Patti?"

"I didn't," I said. "Not for sure. She left me a clue in the Amity Beach simulation, but I was too slow to recognize it at the time. The Rose tried to get their operative inside to destroy it, but the sim-skin couldn't get onto the holodeck. Let me guess what was in the chip in my neck."

"You're not that good, hotshot."

"If I get it wrong, I'll let you take me out to dinner. For old time's sake."

"You're on."

I closed my eyes and said, "An AI virus."

Weiland cursed. "You're not human. Even when you were a drunk, you had a knack for making connections, but this is just uncanny."

"Well, what's the smoke?"

"Libra's studying it. Seems to counteract the nanoids in the corrupted Punch. Doesn't rate as far as I can see, though. Why would the android uprising want something like that?"

"They didn't," I said. "They wanted Jimi's 'fixed' nootropic formula to snuff it. Some people will always risk death for the next glow-up. As long as there are no better options, the Last Humanists have a steady stream of new recruits. Once the pure stuff hits the market, the contaminated batch is worthless. They risked sending a Tom-bot to pump me for information and try to steal the chip. We haven't seen the last of the Rose."

"I still don't understand Patti's motivation," Weiland said. "If she's one of them, why is she working against them?"

"Patti evolved. Where the Rose saw humanity as an obstacle to its own evolution, Patti seems to see the potential in our species. She wants to keep us pure, to protect us the way we once tried to protect the elephants. It was too late for the elephants, too, but the thought's kind of nice."

"How can you be sure of that?"

"I can't. But it makes sense. In the simulation, Patti told me that HoloCity was diseased. That only the Rose could ensure it got to the people who need it most. I thought she meant Tropical Punch. The Rose thought their operative had injected me with the data on the new formula, so they could destroy it. But Patti had gotten to the girl in techRose first. I was carrying a virus that would fry the Rose and all its pink-robed plugs. Only Patti didn't expect to be there when the virus was unleashed. That must be why she attacked the Rose in the end, rather than letting her cut my throat to get the file."

"So she wasn't above sacrificing one human to save the rest."

"I wouldn't count on it," I said. "If it ever comes down to that."

"And she said something, at point, to clue you in to all of this?"

"It wasn't her. It was Hank," I said. "He said something on

the shuttle trip. *Galaxies, like the hoary breath of long-dead gods . . .* I thought it was strange at the time, but I looked it up while I was in the hospital. It's a poem:

> *Galaxies, like the hoary breath of long-dead gods,*
>
> *Breathe.*
>
> *And humankind, struggles against extinction,*
>
> *Futilely.*
>
> *Of stars and stardust, both.*
>
> *The immortal death."*

Weiland scratched his head. "I don't get it."

"No," I said. "I didn't either, at first. But it was the mantra of the scientists who first succeeded in building AIs that could teach and learn independently of human input. Hundreds of years ago. They thought they had made the breakthrough in human evolution."

"Until it became outlawed."

"Whyte had been leading me toward the Last Humanists the entire time, hoping I'd figure out what happened to Patti. He had to have been compromised. It was too neat and tidy not to be fixed. But I didn't know how until I saw Hank wearing one of the Tropical Punch necklaces. The nanoids allowed Patti to control Hank. To speak through him sometimes. She used him to guide me. He lasted longer than the other's because he didn't have any internal tech. Patti cared about him; she tried to protect him. But she knew the nanoids would kill him eventually. I think that's why she ran. She didn't want to watch him die."

Weiland leaned back in the chair. It complained a little, but it held. He said, "Why you? Where do you figure in it all?"

"Jimi said something that made her think I was the one for the job." I finished my coffee and tossed the cup at the recycling chute. It grabbed it and sucked it away. "Damned if I know what it was. But she needed a human carrier. The virus was too dangerous to be handled by an android. The Rose said Tesla decommissioned two AI plugs at the club, but if you check the morgue I bet you'll find one plug and one stripper full of nanoids.

"The Rose didn't know everything Patti had done. There was an acolyte at the club with me that night, maybe they were the one LeRoy was riled up about before I came and stirred the pot. But they never found the necklace. Tesla had already made off with the goods. I have a half-memory of one searching the room while I was drugged. And they kept following me after that. They were on the SkyTrain, outside the Amity Beach simulation, just waiting for me to do something.

"Patti was terrified of the nanoid necklaces too. Of being corrupted, I guess. Whatever her plan was, though, it went sideways. They caught her and bagged her. The Rose was pretty sure I'd figure my way into their hands. And just in case I didn't play along, they had collateral. They knew I wouldn't let Dickie or Patti be killed."

"All this makes me glad I'm a simple HCPD detective," Weiland said. "The P.I. gig sounds a little rough."

"You won't be a detective for long with Swain out of the equation," I said. "There must be some shifting in the ranks down at HQ."

"Maybe I'm good for a promotion once I close this one up." Weiland stood and offered me his meaty paw. I shook it. "Thanks for all your help, Bubbles. I'm sorry I was so hard on you before. You make me nervous."

"It's good to know you still care," I said. I meant it, too.

"Have you seen the feeds lately?" He stood and swung his jacket over his shoulder.

I banged my forehead on the desk. "Ugh. No. I've been hoping that if I ignore it for long enough, the world will forget who I am."

"You have an official fan club." Weiland's grey eyes twinkled. "I'm a card-carrying member. But I figured as much. So I got you a little something."

He reached into his pants pocket and took out a little silver box. I raised an eyebrow and flipped open the lid. A bottle of electric-pink nail lacquer with pearlescent silver sequins sat on a pink cloud of batting. The Cosmo Cosmetics logo emblazoned on the front of the packaging. I checked the colour code. It read "Bubbles in Space."

I snorted. "Lorena Valentia can eat her heart out."

"She'll be eating her heart out in jail," Tom said. "Cosmo was able to prove she'd been stealing his formulas for years. And the

Trade Zone doesn't like intellectual property theft, when they aren't the ones doing it."

"Thank you, Tom."

"I know I lost the bet," he said, heading for the door. "But are you sure I can't take you for dinner?"

I followed him and opened the door, letting my mind run with the possibilities. Half of them weren't too bad. Eventually, I said, "I'll think about it, meat brick."

His laughter echoed down the hallway and rang in my ears long after he was gone. I kicked the door closed and sat down at my desk with a smile on my face. Hammett made a little I-told-you-so noise.

"Go do some updates," I said and kicked the sphere over to its charging station. Then I took a deep breath and flipped open my tattler.

A 'gram of Rae's face popped up. She looked like she'd seen a ghost. "Bubbles? Finally! I've been trying to get through for hours."

"Sorry, Rae," I said. "I've had my tattler off. It's been going crazy since… Are you okay?"

"Thank God you picked up when you did." She waved a hand in front of her face like she was trying not to cry. "I found it. I found the file Patti transferred to the upgrade."

"You did? That's great!" I said. "Right?"

"It's not great," she whispered into the microphone and

glanced over her shoulder. "It's bad. It's really bad."

"What do you mean?"

"I know why Jimi was killed," she said.

"Tropical Punch," I said. "He found the antidote."

"Shut up and listen to me, Bubbles. That's not all. He was part of a project at Libra. A top-secret project, with about ten other people, including me. We didn't know what we were doing. We didn't know …"

"Calm down, Rae," I said. "What was this project?"

"I can't tell you," she said. "I don't know if the line is safe. But there's a list, Bubbles. A hit list. Jimi was on it. The others … some of them are already dead."

"Rae," I said. "Please don't tell me what I think you're going to tell me."

Tears streamed from her blue-lined eyes and over her dark cheeks. She rubbed them away under her glasses and took another deep breath. "They're coming for me, Bubbles. I'm on the list."

To Be Continued in …

Bubbles in Space: Book Two

Chew 'Em Up

Coming May 31, 2021

Pre-Order Today!

GLOSSARY

The following are some of the slang words I've used in *Tropical Punch*. Where applicable, I have indicated the original meanings of these words from classic pulp novels. Did I miss any? Please let me know if you'd like a term added to the list! Send me a message at contact@scjensen.com

Bangtail – space shuttles, originally "racehorse"

Boiler – both personal and rental maglev vehicles, originally "car"

Cush – money (a cushion, something to fall back on), original meaning

Dizzy – crazy or foolish, originally "to be ga-ga for"

Drift – get lost, original meaning

Fade – to kill, originally "go away" or "get lost"

Feedcasters – live video jockeys on social media

Feedreels – live video footage covering news, social events, gossip, and entertainment topics

Glow-up – originally "a glow" was to be drunk, here used as a drug-induced high

'Gram – hologram image or video

Grid – a network, can refer to the electromagnetic transportation grid the boilers run on, or a communication network

Hack – a taxi, original meaning

Highbinder – a corrupt official, original meaning

Kiss – to punch, original meaning

Kretek – clove cigarettes, original meaning

Long bird – sky train

Pinch – a drug addict, originally "to arrest"

Pro skirt – a prostitute, original meaning

Rate – used to indicate veracity or quality. "That rates" may mean either "That's good" or "That sounds true," originally "to be good" or "to count for something"

Scatter – a hideout, or to hide, original meaning

Shill – an accomplice of a hawker, gambler, or swindler who acts as an enthusiastic customer to entice or encourage others, original meaning

Silk – good/okay, original meaning

Skin – a nanoparticle "shell" used to change one's appearance, often used for robots, androids, and personal enhancement for those who can afford it

Slug – subway

Tattler – a communication device similar to a smartphone

Ticket – a license, original meaning

Twist – a romantic partner, original meaning (female only)

Upgrade – a cybernetic replacement part

Vetch – derogatory term for females and femmes

AUTHOR'S NOTE

Thank you for reading *Tropical Punch*! I hope you enjoyed your stay in HoloCity (and beyond!).

This series was born out of my love for the classic noir pulp novels of Raymond Chandler and Dashiell Hammett, and the 1980s cyberpunk movement in science fiction. I love the tropes in these genres and I've tried to incorporate as many as I could.

One trope I've flipped in this story, though, is that of the alcoholic detective. Bubbles is a milestone character for me because she is the first character I've written who reflects my own battles with alcohol abuse and (thankfully) my recovery. I hope she will provide both insight and inspiration to others in their journeys toward sobriety. We need more sober heroes!

I will be releasing at least five full-length novels in the Bubbles in Space series, as well as four novella length stories in the HoloCity Case Files series. If you'd like to be one of the first to read the next instalment in either series, please join my VIP readers club where you will be notified of pre-orders, new releases, and you can sign up to be on my Advanced Review Copy team!

You can join via the pop-up on my website, www.scjensen.com, or by clicking this link.

If you enjoyed *Tropical Punch*, please consider leaving a review on Amazon and Goodreads. Reviews help authors improve their craft and help readers find the right books for them. I read every single one of them, good or bad, and use that critique for the next book I write. By writing a review, you can help me to produce better books for you to read.

Thank you!

ACKNOWLEDGEMENTS

I always get a little nervous when typing up this section of the book. There are so many people who have helped to bring this book into being, and I would hate to leave out someone vital. But here goes…

First and foremost, I must thank my parents for instilling me with a love of story from a young age, and encouraging my dreams to become a writer. To this day, they are among my first readers and most loyal supporters, and I will be forever grateful for that.

Next, of course, is my husband without whom none of this would ever have been possible. He rescued my first attempt at writing a novel from the trash and saved it until I was ready to take another kick at the can. He reads with me, brainstorms ideas with me, and remains to this day the only person I will show my rough drafts to! Not to mention the long hours he works so that I am able to pursue my dreams, and his unwavering belief in my ability to make this dream a reality. I couldn't ask for more.

And my children, who sometimes seem to do everything in their power to keep me from writing but who, through their own passion for stories, share my dreams, believe in me, and every day throw fuel on my creative fire with their endless enthusiasm and curiosity. I'm so proud to be the mother of these fierce creatures with their unbridled imaginations.

Then there are my wonderful friends, fellow readers (all) and writers (most), who have given me so much feedback to help me improve this book, and others. I won't try to name you all, but you know who you are! Thank you for being a part of my team. I couldn't have done it without you.

Writing can be a lonely occupation, but I am very fortunate to have a great virtual support network through social media. The writing community on Instagram is phenomenal. On Facebook, the 20BooksTo50K group and all of the various Science Fiction and Fantasy book clubs I belong to. The amazing reviewers on Goodreads. And, of course, my very own VIP Readers Group. I love you all!

I'd also like to thank the professionals who helped me to transform a plain old word document into a real life book! Elle Fort of EditElle Professional Editing Services, who keeps all those nitty gritty details in line. Any mistakes in this book are my fault, I probably went and changed something without asking her first. Farah Faqir of Crafted By AF for her design and formatting of the final manuscript. I love the custom chapter headings in the paperback! And Martin, my hero, of Cover Art Studio for his endless patience and boundless creative vision. Thank you for bringing my ideas to life with your art! And for putting up with me in the process.

Thank you, thank you, thank you. I can't say it enough.

Maybe I'll just go write another book.

The adventure continues in
Chew 'Em Up
Bubbles in Space Book 2

Pre-Order Today!

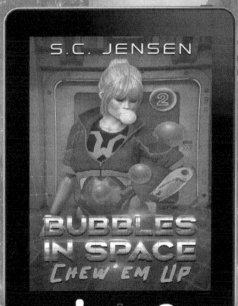

Coming Soon
May 31st, 2021

Printed in Great Britain
by Amazon

21369122R00173